One-way str[eet]

They had just nego[tiated the]
night of the tunnel [when it]
started spitting orange flames fr[om...]

Aussie, the temporary Phoenix Force pilot, had taken the lead and now gave a low cry. Katz pressed forward to reach the injured man's side and managed to get behind him. But bullets still plowed through the sticky darkness, and Katz could do nothing further beyond flattening himself on the ground.

"Shoot for the muzzle-flash!" the Australian yelled unexpectedly. His voice blended into a howl of rage, then into silence just as Katz steeled himself for the angry sting of bullets. Suddenly a strange comprehension hit the Phoenix leader—the big man's bulk before him...the narrowness of the tunnel...

"Hell," Katz muttered, and there was a bitter taste in his mouth. He'd come to like the man and had developed a grudging respect for his brash and pushy style. "Aussie," he whispered, and gave him a nudge. "Aussie, you all right?" he asked with forlorn hope, but his voice seemed to be swallowed by that black hellhole.

Mack Bolan's
PHOENIX FORCE.

- #1 Argentine Deadline
- #2 Guerilla Games
- #3 Atlantic Scramble
- #4 Tigers of Justice
- #5 The Fury Bombs
- #6 White Hell
- #7 Dragon's Kill
- #8 Aswan Hellbox
- #9 Ultimate Terror
- #10 Korean Killground
- #11 Return to Armageddon
- #12 The Black Alchemists
- #13 Harvest Hell
- #14 Phoenix in Flames
- #15 The Viper Factor
- #16 No Rules, No Referee
- #17 Welcome to the Feast
- #18 Night of the Thuggee
- #19 Sea of Savages
- #20 Tooth and Claw
- #21 The Twisted Cross
- #22 Time Bomb
- #23 Chip Off the Bloc
- #24 The Doomsday Syndrome
- #25 Down Under Thunder
- #26 Hostaged Vatican
- #27 Weep, Moscow, Weep
- #28 Slow Death
- #29 The Nightmare Merchants
- #30 The Bonn Blitz
- #31 Terror in the Dark
- #32 Fair Game
- #33 Ninja Blood
- #34 Power Gambit
- #35 Kingston Carnage
- #36 Belgrade Deception
- #37 Show of Force
- #38 Missile Menace
- #39 Jungle Sweep
- #40 Rim of Fire

PHOENIX FORCE.

GAR WILSON

RIM OF FIRE

A GOLD EAGLE BOOK FROM
WORLDWIDE.

TORONTO · NEW YORK · LONDON · PARIS
AMSTERDAM · STOCKHOLM · HAMBURG
ATHENS · MILAN · TOKYO · SYDNEY

First edition March 1989

ISBN 0-373-61340-7

Special thanks and acknowledgment to
Dan Streib for his contribution to this work.

Copyright © 1989 by Worldwide Library.
Philippine copyright 1989. Australian copyright 1989.

All rights reserved. Except for use in any review, the
reproduction or utilization of this work in whole or in part
in any form by any electronic, mechanical or other means,
now known or hereafter invented, including xerography,
photocopying and recording, or in any information storage
or retrieval system, is forbidden without the permission
of the publisher, Worldwide Library, 225 Duncan Mill Road,
Don Mills, Ontario, Canada M3B 3K9.

All the characters in this book have no existence outside the
imagination of the author and have no relation whatsoever to
anyone bearing the same name or names. They are not even
distantly inspired by any individual known or unknown to the
author, and all incidents are pure invention.

® are Trademarks registered in the United States Patent and
Trademark Office and in other countries.

Printed in U.S.A.

1

From the air at night, Cairo's City of the Dead appears to some travelers as an ominous black void in a sprawling array of sparkling lights.

To others, it seems a gigantic oil spill that smothers everything beneath its surface. It could also be mistaken for a bottomless pit or a stretch of treacherous quicksand.

On Air Force One the Vice President of the United States, Stephen Shaw, could not keep from staring at the massive blot.

He thought of the bodies there.

Although he was perfectly safe, and American and Egyptian jet fighters flew ahead, behind and on either side of his aircraft, he felt apprehensive.

Now, with the flying command ship dropping toward the Egyptian military airfield, Shaw could see the outlines of buildings and the network of the city's dark, narrow, foreboding streets.

It was truly a city within a city, a vast neighborhood for the dead.

In an area capable of housing thousands of Egyptians without crowding, not a single light shone. It was a city of ghosts and gargoyles. And he was being drawn into it by some mysterious force he could not grasp.

Surrounding the City of the Dead, Cairo glistened, a lively and cruel contrast of modern glass skyscrapers and ancient mud huts.

Cairo, the capital of the north African nation of fifty million Arabs, lay one hundred miles south of the Mediterranean, straddling the Nile where the life-sustaining river divided like fingers before reaching the sea.

From his high-backed executive chair in the flying office, Vice President Shaw looked out at the river stretching through the desert. It was, he knew, a formidable force: a life-giving agent that irrigated the thirsty desert, a killer when she lost control.

Most of Egypt's population lived within a few miles of the river, which had its origins in the distant wetlands of southern Africa.

Desert crept across much of the rest of the continent.

As Shaw peered through the windows, a buzzer sounded, and his brow furrowed.

"Sir."

Shaw ignored the voice and the percussive click of knuckles on the door to the presidential airborne office.

He continued to stare out the oval window.

"Sir." The knock sounded again. "Mr. Vice President."

Warily, Shaw checked the video monitor over the door. It displayed two men on the other side of the paneling.

He recognized both: one was a Secret Service man, the other Army Major Allen Lukes, formerly known as Ali Mamelukes. That name went back aeons, to the time of Turkish slaves who had come to rule Egypt. He had anglicized it before entering the military academy. The dossier prepared for the VP mentioned Caucasian features, including blue eyes and skin of a color between Nordic white and olive drab.

Stephen Shaw was suspicious of people who changed their names.

"Sir? Are you all right in there?" The agent tried the door handle. It did not budge until Shaw released the latch on the control panel in the arm of his chair.

The Army major entered. The Secret Service agent peered into the lavishly furnished compartment, then closed the door.

Shaw was not a tall man. Friendly newscasters made him appear taller than his five-foot-eight stature. The gray in his hair made him look older than his forty-eight years. His strong face bore a scar across the left cheek, a silent reminder to his constituents of his POW days in Vietnam. A smart publicity agent tied the scar to the Medal of Honor Shaw had won for single-handedly repelling more than fifty Vietcong from his retreating platoon.

In a month he would be sworn in as President. He had won the election handily. In thirty days he would lead the most powerful nation in history.

Tonight, his hands shook. Looking at them, he remembered the day he had been captured outside Saigon. His hands had been steady while he waited for the enemy to kill him or save him as a bargaining chip.

Tonight, two decades later, he was afraid.

"Sir," barked Major Lukes, "I am unable to remove the City of the Dead from the itinerary."

"Someone is determined to get me in there," Shaw said as the plane lowered and the City of the Dead dissolved in Cairo's glitter. He glanced at the major's sidearm, a ceremonial silver piece with a tank carved into the ivory handles.

It somehow made Shaw uneasy that the major was allowed to carry a gun in his presence. Was this man, who spoke Arabic fluently and who was to be a valet to the President-elect until they left the Arab world, completely trustworthy?

"I don't understand the problem," the stocky officer said. "The Egyptians are proud to have discovered Arab blood in your ancestry. They researched for a month to discover that your maternal great great-grandfather's brother rests in the City of the Dead. They want you to visit the tomb."

"I never heard any of my relatives speak of an Egyptian in the family tree."

"Even if it's a mistake..."

"A lie, you mean."

"All right, it may be a lie. But we are not here to call our hosts liars. Besides, you'll be surrounded by guards."

"Egyptian guards," said Shaw. "Any one of whom might be a suicidal fanatic."

The major said, "If the embassy calls the president of Egypt in the middle of the night to protest a routine tour, we're liable to cause an international incident."

"Routine tour?" The Vice President laughed. "First, we stop at the reviewing stand where Anwar Sadat was assassinated, then visit the pyramids for pictures of me coming out of some pharaoh's tomb. Then we go to the City of the Dead for TV coverage of me walking through streets lined with palatial homes inhabited by corpses. All at night. The whole thing is morbid."

"Sir, refusing to admit you have Muslim ancestry would be insulting."

"To you? You changed your Arab name."

The major was silent.

"You're part Arab, aren't you?"

"Yes, sir."

Shaw smiled. "Are you still dealing with the protocol officer at the embassy?" he asked.

"Yes, sir."

"What's his name?"

"Leonard Toby."

Shaw remembered hearing the name before. "Toby. Hell, he's CIA. We're getting as bad as the Russians, filling our embassies with espionage agents. Forget him. Talk to the ambassador."

"We can't reach him, sir. He's probably at the airport, awaiting your arrival. Besides, he's already tried diplomatically to change your itinerary." Major Lukes took a deep breath. "Sir, we've got to keep this on a low level."

"Try again," the VP told the major.

"But, sir..."

"You have all day tomorrow," the Vice President interrupted. "And don't ruffle any feathers."

"But your request will more than ruffle a few feathers, sir."

"Do the best you can," Shaw persisted. He closed his eyes, effectively ending the conversation.

Minutes before he had sworn he would not capitulate. He would be damned if he would visit the dead.

Now, with the black hole in the city behind him, he laughed at his own ridiculous fears.

He did not open his eyes until he heard the door close.

His fears were ridiculous, especially since they had been triggered by a half-crazed fortune-teller. As he had stepped from the President's limousine at the airport in Washington, a young woman dressed as a Gypsy had slipped through the elaborate security wall and spoken to him in a voice that befitted one of Shakespeare's witches.

"Stay away from the dead," she had said. "Far away. Do you hear?"

Security agents had wrestled her to the ground and dragged her away for interrogation.

It all seemed so ridiculous now. And so far away.

They passed over the heart of Cairo and there were lights, a million of them at least. The clear sky sparkled with stars. The bright airport runways and the modernistic terminal were ready to cheerfully greet him. There would be a red carpet and a band despite the midnight arrival.

He found his briefing file and began to read.

Egypt. A civilization that stretches back five thousand years. The first to organize a national government. The first to believe in a life after death. Egyptians introduced papyrus, first convenient material on which to write. The first to use the 365-day calendar. The first to use geometry. The first to perform surgery.

His interest in the subject overtook the fear that had been in his mind.

The City of the Dead, he thought. It's nothing but a cemetery.

2

The helicopter swooped low, its down draft bending the tops of the stately old pines. The chopper dropped toward the camouflaged airstrip and hovered two or three feet above the ground.

Hal Brognola leaped from the cargo door and landed on the run. The chopper climbed sharply, leaving him no reason to stoop to avoid the blades.

In the foothills of the northeast, the cool air and the scent of pine normally soothed Hal Brognola's nerves. He appreciated Stony Man Farm with its large house, always freshly painted, it seemed. The outbuildings were always in repair and in the summer the lawn rarely went a week without being mowed.

Today, though, nothing soothed him. He had been on the run since he left the White House on a chopper that carried him to the airport.

Chewing at an unlit cigar, he rushed through the familiar landscape on his way to the house.

The farm was a miniature Pentagon, a headquarters for a tiny army that sometimes outperformed full military divisions. It was equipped with a complete military support system of underground bunkers and camouflaged training facilities, a storehouse of guns, ammo, currency, passports and files of phony identities. A secret communications complex could put Brognola in touch with his agents regardless of where they were on earth.

"Just another mission," he told himself. But he knew there was no such thing as an easy mission for the men he directed from the Farm.

This time the particulars of the situation especially worried him.

The target was an elusive one. He would be asking his men to go up against a fierce, unidentified foe, without time to plan or properly arm themselves.

With that on his mind, he entered the house and went directly to the War Room. He pressed a button beside the conference table to activate a wall chart. The map, dotted with lights and pins, was of the entire world. It showed where Russian military units were deployed, and replicas of submarines and ships, with surprising accuracy, marked the positions of the world's navies. It also showed the size and location of the nuclear arsenals on both sides of the Iron Curtain.

Brognola searched for five small flashing lights, each representing a Phoenix Force agent.

The team Brognola commanded had demonstrated an amazing combat ability.

It had saved the Vatican when the holy state's remarkable Swiss Guards had failed.

It had sneaked across national boundaries where no army dared to go. It had silently removed more than one madman from a dangerous position of power.

Bound by no law except their own internal sense of fairness, justice and honor, the five men of Phoenix

Force served the American President upon request. They retained the independence they needed to grind evil under their boots wherever they found it.

In short, they were created in the image of Mack Bolan, a.k.a. the Executioner, who had declared war on the Mafia and won, and who squelched terrorists wherever he found them.

Today Hal Brognola was under presidential orders.

"Put Phoenix Force on this immediately. We might not get a chance like this again," the President had decreed.

Brognola touched the green button and waited.

"DOES THE NAME *Sadam* mean anything to you?"

Yakov Katzenelenbogen dropped the radiophone.

Hal Brognola was shouting. "Katz? Where the hell are you? What's going on?"

"Sorry."

"Can you hear me okay? Sometimes the phone link between stateside and Israel isn't that great. I asked if you've heard of a character named Sadam."

"Don't shout, I hear you loud and clear. Of course I know of Sadam. Who doesn't? He's hijacked five jets, two ships. Helped kill eleven Israeli athletes at the Munich Olympics. Plus he nearly toppled the Eiffel Tower and the Washington Monument."

"His men did all that and more," Brognola said. "So far he's never been seen or heard. Some think he doesn't really exist."

"He's real," Katz said. "Secret leaders require one tough, loyal associate. Sadam probably works through one lieutenant."

"Kamal," Brognola said. "Nahib Kamal."

"You know Sadam's second in command?"

"We know the name. CIA, NSA, FBI, Interpol and God knows who else, are all working together to put a history to this Kamal."

"You find him, we'll skewer Sadam at a barbecue on the Farm."

"I think I know where Kamal is headed," the man from the Farm added. Katz felt himself stiffen.

"Where?"

"We know that members of Sadam's private army sneaked through the Sinai Peninsula, crossed the Suez Canal and are probably headed for Cairo. We figure Kamal, if not Sadam himself, must be with them."

Katz recollected a headline he had recently read: *Vice President Shaw Is Headed for Cairo.*

"Kamal's there already," he told Brognola. "You want us to protect Shaw?"

"Yes and no. The Secret Service and the Egyptians are responsible for our top dogs. But Kamal and Sadam are another matter. We want them, Katz, before..."

"Before they kill Vice President Shaw."

"Yes."

"Where do you want us to go?" Katz was ready to receive his orders. He was absolutely loyal to Phoenix Force. Everything else could manage without him.

"Cairo. The pyramids. There's a fabulous light show at sunset. Climb to the top of the Cheops pyramid. I'll arrange it so you don't get your tail shot off by some local cop. You'll have a good view from there.

And if Sadam's people do make a strike, they'll come in from the desert rather than from the city."

"You're calling in the others, right?"

"Right."

"We rendezvous at the same place."

"Okay."

"We'll need a helicopter. Nobody gets around Cairo fast enough on the ground."

"It'll be there. And I'm giving you a local guide."

"I prefer just the team members."

"He knows Cairo. He chased Sadam before. He thinks he could recognize Kamal if he saw him. Give him a try. Drop him whenever you want."

"Okay. What about weapons? Should we bring our own?"

"No. You might get tripped up at the border. Aussie—he's your guide—will have everything you need."

"You're contacting the others?" Katz asked.

"Right. And Katz, be careful." Instantly Brognola was gone.

PHOENIX FORCE AGENT David McCarter sat behind the wheel of a twelve-foot-high pickup truck. Huge tires held the vehicle so high that a man could walk underneath. It was part of a fast-growing fad: pickup trucks, regular size and loaded to the roll bars with weight, mounted on giant wheels that weighed tons and tons.

McCarter was in the San Diego Sports Arena. Thousands of fans filled the stands. They wanted to see power. To see the monsters crush everything in their path.

McCarter doubted if the fans understood their own lust. But they loved seeing regular passenger cars flattened beneath the monstrous wheels.

Ahead of him now were six old standard-sized cars in a line. At the far end was a new Cadillac.

The enormous tires began to move. A driver of anything with spirit, he reveled in the power and the fierce roar of the engine. He loved racing because it tested man and machine. He field-tested new cars because he could take them to their limit, make sure they were ready for the market.

Many people thought of David McCarter as an easygoing man. But he was deeply suspicious, a man who survived by his strength and his ruthless wit. And he had tuned all his body systems so well he could thumb his nose at danger. He was doing that now, thumbing his nose at the power he could control.

The heavy tires left two-inch-deep arrow tracks in the hard-packed dirt of the arena. Shifting to help the seven-hundred-horsepower engine, McCarter did not break his concentration as a telephone rang. He had one on the dash as his link with the men guiding him from outside, but he ignored it.

One wrong turn of the wheel and the mechanical elephant could overturn and flatten like a waffle in spite of the sturdy roll bars.

The audience began getting to their feet. A few shouted encouragement.

When the sound of the phone changed pitch, he knew the call was from Stony Man.

"Yeah?" he said with only twenty yards left between him and the first of the cars.

"I bought you a present," Hal Brognola said from the dash speaker. "A ticket to the sound-and-light show in Cairo."

"The pyramids?"

The monster had reached the first car. McCarter could still hear Brognola over the sounds of cracking glass and grinding iron. But his hands and thoughts were primarily locked on the problem with the first car. It was not collapsing evenly. If he continued, the crusher might roll off.

"Yes. Tomorrow night. Just after dark sets in."

"Hell." He brought his vehicle to a halt.

He knew who was in Cairo. Vice President Shaw. He did not try to guess how that involved him.

"Rendezvous at the pinnacle of the biggest pyramid," Brognola said. "Sadam might be there."

"Sadam?" Brognola now had his full attention.

"Yes."

Then Brognola signed off.

McCarter's volatile temper flared. Surprising the crowd and his own crew, he shifted into reverse and backed off the first car. He did not stop until his rear bumper nearly touched the bleachers.

He gunned the engine, spraying the first two rows of seats with dirt. The crowd rose as he picked up speed. Mechanics shouted warnings.

McCarter crushed the first car on the run, the sound of crackling metal competing with the cheering crowd.

The second vehicle flattened just as easily. McCarter rolled over the next vehicles more slowly, preparing for the pickup truck at the end of the line, before the Cadillac.

For McCarter, the thrill of the challenge meant all. All the crackling and breaking and tearing beneath meant nothing to him. The crowd could have all gone home as far as he was concerned.

The monster flattened the pickup track, the giant tires moving relentlessly over the wreck of metal and glass.

"Hey, you bloody machine, we're doing it!" he shouted as the rear wheels dropped onto the Cadillac. The monster was off balance. He knew he was going to crash, but he was bursting with pleasure as he flattened the new car before beginning the roll.

Fear grabbed him briefly and he felt the roof of the monster crushing in on him. Mercifully, fate stole his consciousness.

He awoke on the stretcher with four burly truck drivers rushing him from the arena to a waiting ambulance. The crowd was silent until he slid off the stretcher and waved as his carriers were putting him inside the red-and-white emergency vehicle.

"Thanks for the ride, blokes," he said, in spite of a thundering headache. "I can manage from here." He seemed indifferent to the blood dripping into his eyes.

He glanced at the wreckage he had left behind and exited the arena on unsteady knees while the crowd applauded him like a gladiator who had escaped the lion.

RAFAEL ENCIZO SAT at the blackjack table in the Casino Rios, Puerto Rico's newest, most lavish gambling den for the tourists and the rich island locals.

He had a hundred dollars in chips on the rectangle in front of him, but he remained expressionless as he flipped over an ace and a black queen.

"No," he said to the men sitting on either side of him. He lapsed into Spanish. "No more Bay of Pigs."

He was the shortest of the five Phoenix Force agents at five feet eight inches, and the lightest by far at 158 pounds.

Nothing about his appearance described the man inside. His black hair was grizzled, his eyes a neutral brown. His face was squarish with a strong suggestion of Indian genes: flat nose, heavy brows, strong forehead, deeply clefted chin.

His stocky muscular build and powerful biceps deceived people he met; they perceived a slow man of lethargic intellect.

Nothing on the outside told of his youth in the mountains where he fought alongside Fidel Castro for Cuban freedom. He had chosen the winning side only to learn he had helped install a dictator as bad as, or worse than, the one they had overthrown. Resisting the slide into communism cost him years in Castro prisons.

Now the two Cubans with him were trying to solicit his help with another invasion of their homeland. They were good men, civic leaders in Miami, but their cause was hopeless.

Encizo wanted no part of the idea.

He welcomed the interruption when a security guard stepped up to him and said, "You have a phone call from your farm manager, Mr. Encizo."

"Gracias," Encizo said as he collected his chips. "Sorry," he told the two men before excusing himself.

He put the phone to his ear, and heard Brognola give him instructions at machine-gun speed.

"There's an Air Force plane leaving in thirty-five minutes for Cairo. Be on it."

"Wait. Not so fast, amigo."

"You'll get there just in time to see the show at sunset tomorrow."

"What show?"

"The light show at the pyramids. Your friends will be waiting for you near the top of the Cheops pyramid. And perhaps Sadam will be there, too."

"Bueno."

Encizo returned the phone to the hook, and quietly slipped out of the casino.

CALVIN JAMES, at twenty-nine Phoenix Force's youngest member, coughed and gasped for air. His eyes watered. He could squint through one eye at a time, for two or three seconds at most.

James had fought a lot in his life. Bullet wounds on his rib cage had left their mark, and there was a knife cut on his right hand that he had suffered while fighting in the streets of Chicago as a kid. A black American, he had recently allied himself with the equal-rights movement in South Africa.

Today he withstood tear gas with several thousand mine workers who were battling for a bigger housing project in South Africa. While the mine owners had recently built hundreds of small homes, thousands of the black laborers lived in unisex dormitories. Their families lived hundred of miles away, and the men often went a year without seeing their wives and children.

The high-pressure water cannons were on their way. The police were loading their riot guns with rubber bullets.

So the sudden surge of blacks would be their last.

"Charge!" someone shouted.

As if on command, the mob raced forward. They threw what projectiles they had left and picked up more when the police retreated. Calvin James fought with the crowd. He wanted the demonstrators to know that there were Americans in sympathy with their cause.

Then a wood bullet grazed his head, stunning him. He landed on his rear. The crowd nearly trampled him, first during the charge, and again in retreat.

He was trying to get to his feet when his tiny, portable communication device in his pocket beeped.

From the sound of his voice, James imagined that Hal Brognola was puzzled over the background noises. Gunfire snapped above the shouting. Tear gas canisters hissed. The sound of cracking skulls punctuated the screams of pain as police whacked the bodies of blacks with heavy wooden batons. Then the water truck came into range.

"What's happening there?" Brognola demanded.

As James explained, he was knocked down by a column of water.

"Well, forget the water slide and get to Cairo by tomorrow," Brognola said. He gave James the same instructions he had given the others.

"Sadam." Calvin James felt great. Sadam presented a bigger challenge than what he was doing now. "I'll be there," he said. "Don't worry. These guys don't really need me."

Yeah, he thought.

Sadam was his kind of adversary.

GARY MANNING, the Canadian team member, sat in a rowboat propelled by a trolling motor. He had a fifteen-pound northern pike on the line when Hal Brognola reached him.

"Manning?" the Stony Man Farm manager asked. "What's that hissing sound I hear?"

"A northern pike taking out line against the drag."

"What? Never mind."

Manning struggled to reel in the fish, maneuver the net and avoid toppling into the lake while carrying on a conversation with Brognola. Fortunately, the man at the Farm was terse with his orders.

"Get to any Air Force base, Canadian or American. Contact me from there. I'll have clearance for you to ride in the rear seat of the fastest jet they have ready to go. Got that?"

"Yes, but where am I going?"

"Cairo. The pyramid back of the Sphinx. Just after dark. Be near the top."

Manning felt the surge of excitement that usually

streaked through his body when he got a chance to practice his trade.

Still, he grumbled, "Damn."

The huge northern pike boiled on the surface and then he was gone.

3

Mohammed Sadam and his twenty men were concealed by the slight rise in the barren land east of Cairo.

They were all on their bellies, but only Sadam wore a white cloth wrapped around his head and pulled across his face, so that just his icy-blue eyes and brown eyebrows were exposed. Only one man in his growing army had ever seen Sadam's full face. Few had ever heard him speak.

But legions of Arabs had begun to proclaim him as their savior. Thousands were training to join his fledgling army.

In the minds of ruling Arabs, however, he was a threat. They knew his expressed intention.

He wanted a nation he could rule. A large and powerful country, if possible. A small but oil-rich nation would suffice.

Now Sadam placed the butt of a Desert Eagle Magnum in his left hand while his right wrapped around the dark metal grip. His finger touched the trigger affectionately.

Forty yards away, an elderly peasant rode on a camel that grudgingly plodded along the back road to the city. Its hooves landed silently in the noiseless moonscape.

Camels could survive without food for days in the desert. They could do with minimal amounts of water, and were the ideal means of transportation and beasts of burden for many centuries in that kind of environment.

A cantankerous animal, the camel. It hated everything and everyone. It expressed itself by spitting or kicking, but when necessary it could provide meat with the taste of veal. It grew woolly fur that could be woven into cloth. The skin was suitable for shoes. Dried bones could be carved into jewelry or eating utensils.

The man on the ugly animal lolled drowsily in the saddle.

Sadam squinted down the telescopic sight. His second in command, Nahib Kamal, nervously interfered. "Perhaps it would be better to buy the camel and not kill the man," he said tentatively.

Sadam took his eye from the sight and stared at Kamal. After several moments, he said, "No."

He had left Cairo to join his armed followers. He had stood alone on the small knoll, waiting, a warlock ready to unleash his demons.

He returned to his gun, aiming for the head and leading the target by an inch or two.

It would be easier to fire at the man's torso, but Sadam had special bullets that he wished to try. They were supposed to be silver-jacketed over a soft-lead core. They would expand with particular intensity on impact.

He fired. The man on the camel flew off. His brains exploded out the left side of his head.

"Magnificent," Sadam said. "This is true, eh, Kamal?"

"Yes, Colonel."

Sadam had named himself a colonel because the rank was used by the ruler of Libya. There were no generals, no other colonels. The only other ranks were sergeant, lieutenant, private and untrained recruit.

Several unit commanders came forward to watch as Sadam put five more bullets into the body. The dead man danced under the impact of the rapid fire.

"Shoot," Sadam ordered. "All of you."

They obeyed, and the body twitched and squirmed as the bullets hit.

Good, Sadam thought. It was like a blood oath. Even the new members were legally killers.

"Colonel," said the quietly efficient Kamal, who held the rank of lieutenant. "I think it is time to move the body before another traveler comes along."

Sadam glanced to either side. The raw recruits were peering cautiously over the incline.

The sight of the body warned them. They would be outlaws if they were caught, freedom fighters if they triumphed.

"Yes," Sadam told his aide. "Hide the body. Bring the animal to me. I will ride into Cairo on the camel. I do not want to endanger the others by my presence."

"Yes, Colonel."

The men stood up. Kamal gave the orders, and the others began to mount the old semitrailer truck parked just off the main road that led into the city. One or two might die from the relentless sun and the poor ventilation, but thousands more were in training.

The men in the truck would reach the City of the Dead before nightfall. The colonel would be there before that.

The men thought he lived in some desert oasis between missions. In truth, he stayed at penthouse suites and partied with women. He drank whatever he wanted without threat of punishment; his life was vastly better than it had been in prohibitionist Saudi Arabia.

As the troops left he rode the camel a few miles across the alluvial plain that stretched to the rough landing field and his waiting aircraft.

Against the fluid, modern lines of the jet, Sadam appeared to be an anachronism, a relic of the past. He dressed as a sheikh. He wore an ankle-length shirt of the finest wool. Threads of real gold ran across his shoulders. Three half-inch bands of gold circled the cuff of each sleeve. His turban and the scarf that covered his face were equally ornamented. And he wore a medallion on a heavy gold chain. A curved sword adorned the large gold disk.

Underneath his robe he wore sandals, a white shirt, trousers and a camel-hide belt. In that outfit he would blend into the city population.

Also underneath his robe were his Desert Eagle .44 Magnum and assorted other weapons.

LIEUTENANT NAHIB KAMAL of Sadam's army rode up front with the driver.

The baking sun kept the air hot throughout the long trip to Cairo. The city collected and refused to part with anything, including the heat.

For centuries peasants had expanded the city's rim with mud huts while modern high rises bulged from the center. The garbage dumps became tall hills. People fought for scavenger rights. Modern buses crept through slums while tourists clicked snapshots of the poor, young and old alike.

And the city streets were clogged with traffic despite the new subway. Pedestrians overflowed the sidewalks onto the streets. Donkeys moved as quickly as cars.

The noise never stopped: the cries of peddlers, the wails from the mosque, the rumble and horns of traffic, the rat-a-tat-tat of jackhammers.

Fortunately Lieutenant Kamal did not have to go into the heart of the city. He stopped at the City of the Dead. He had reconnoitered the labyrinth of streets and alleys both inside and outside the vast cemetery.

While leaving the truck, he looked over the lowest part of the wall that bordered parts of the city. His men quickly moved between the miniature stone and mortar mansions.

Over a period of a month, his advanced detachments had been working on the locks of selected tombs. Now two of his men entered each of the stone houses. Although the locks were latched from the outside, the advance men had made certain those inside could get out.

They had not attracted attention. Few people ever entered the dead city. Those who did were squatters who lived in the tombs of their own ancestors. They melted away at the sight of armed young men.

Satisfied that the plan was moving on schedule, Nahib Kamal watched his men enter the magnificently constructed shelter for the crypts. Others shut the doors from the outside and made them appear locked.

Kamal closed in the last two men himself.

He then headed for his observation point, one of many open-air stores that lined one side of the main road passing the City of the Dead.

Several blocks of open-air stands were manned by salesmen who catered to a variety of clientele: they sold postcards and trinkets to tourists who came to see and snap pictures, soda pop or freshly squeezed orange juice for workers who waited for the buses, fruits and vegetables for the few local residents.

Nahib Kamal selected a vegetable stand and approached the old shopkeeper with a smile. *"Tisbah 'ala khair. Kaif halek."*

The old man nodded but a look of distrust appeared on his face.

Kamal said, "I have come to buy your stand."

"I do not wish to sell," the old man said.

"For the right price you will never need to work again."

"Then what do I do with my life?"

Kamal smiled. "Come. We need to discuss this in private."

"Come? Where?"

"Just around the back of the shop. Once you understand how much I am willing to pay, you will agree."

Kamal waited until the old man recognized that he would be forced to sell one way or another.

He led the old merchant behind the stand, where a garbage dump was growing a half foot per day.

Sadam's lieutenant said nothing until they had nearly passed the dump.

There he raised his long shirt and took a knife from the sheath. Although the weapon was unsuited for killing, Kamal drove it into the merchant's abdomen as far as it would go.

The old man opened his mouth to scream, but Kamal clamped his free hand over the man's lips. Making a wide circular cut, he exposed the shopkeeper's internal organs before allowing him to drop.

Propelled by an inner excitement that made his task easy, he dragged the body into the garbage heap and buried it.

When he returned to the shop, the other merchants watched him nervously.

"What happened to the old man?" one of them asked.

"I bought his shop," was the answer.

"I never thought he would give up his trade."

"He was too old for this work," Kamal said. "Now he will live in luxury without work."

"You paid him that well?" one asked.

"Yes. I am a generous man, as you will learn."

4

Vice-President Stephen Shaw zipped himself into a bulletproof vest despite the grueling heat. In a shoulder holster beneath his white jacket, he carried a Beretta Model 950BS with .25 ACP cartridges.

Although the Washington clique frowned on his habit of carrying a defensive weapon, he felt better with his own protection. More than once, as an infantry lieutenant in Vietnam, he had been forced to shoot his way out of a tight situation. From experience he knew that even a platoon of battle-hardened regulars could fall like tenpins.

Today, he trusted the Beretta's straight blow-back action and the open slide design that eliminated jamming. He carried a few extra cartridges in loops sewn into his belt. He liked the tip-up barrel for easy chambering without working the slide.

As he dressed he railed at the three men in his bedroom. "Goddamned incompetency from at least one of you bastards."

"Sir," Major Allen Lukes spoke up sharply. "Sir, I ask for relief from duty. Nobody calls me a bastard."

Shaw stared at him. The man's pride was impressive. "My apologies, Major. But somebody couldn't get a simple change in a motorcade."

"I wasn't informed," the American ambassador sniveled. He came across as a weakling, terrified of losing the only job he could hold.

"Leonard Toby?" Shaw said as he faced the thirty-year-old protocol officer and CIA agent.

"Yes, sir?"

"What's your story?"

"I personally conveyed to the ambassador your request to remove the City of the Dead from the itinerary. I asked repeatedly that he intercede at the highest level."

"Not true," the ambassador whined.

"I have copies of every memo," Toby said.

"Anybody can phony up a copy. You must believe me, Mr. Vice President."

"The copies were made from originals provided by the ambassador's personal secretary."

The ambassador wilted. He sank into a chair.

"Would you like to accompany me to speak personally to the Egyptian president or some other high officer?" Leonard Toby asked Shaw. "Perhaps there is still time to alter the route."

Shaw wanted to say, "Yes." The unreasonable fear still locked itself in his mind. But the car was outside. If he hesitated, he would be late in joining the Egyptian head of state.

"No," he barked. "But I want all three of you to tail us, each in a separate car. Understand?"

"A pleasure," the tall slender Toby said with a smile. "I would be with you in any case."

The other two nodded.

Shaw left the embassy and stalked to the air-conditioned limousine.

Shaw had slept the morning away. After a late lunch, he was starting a tour of government buildings and would begin the ordeal of sight-seeing shortly before dark.

He patted his chest, nervously, checking for the gun.

After Egypt's government offices, he visited the most recently completed stations of Cairo's subway system. His mind ran to New York's equivalent, and he wished he had brought a .357 Magnum. The Egyptian president rode with him from station to station in cars unstained with graffiti and across platforms delightfully cooled with air-conditioning.

The rest of the day was a montage of mosques and banquet halls. By the time the motorcade passed the reviewing stand where Egypt's second president had been gunned down while surrounded by most of the nation's generals, Shaw was groggy with jet lag.

They were behind schedule, and it was dark as the motorcade with police sirens and motorcycle escort entered the complex in front of the Sphinx and the pyramids. Applauding admirers cheered his arrival.

The Sphinx, the statue with the body of a lion and the face of a human, proved smaller than he had expected. It had been carved from solid stone thousands of years ago, supposedly to provide a better view of the pyramids behind it. Shaw was surprised to find that the giant pyramids were not far out in the desert but rather at the very edge of Cairo. A hotel, homes and businesses were close by.

Beyond the ancient stone structures stretched the vast desert.

Shaw wondered how many security people were amid the onlookers. He spotted a few uniformed officers and recognized his own Secret Service men. Three helicopters hovered just above the pyramids, their searchlights combing the desert's edge.

"Only VIPs are in the stands this evening," the Egyptian president told Shaw as he led him to the front row where the flags of both nations flew.

Damn, Shaw thought, his counterpart must have heard of his foolish concerns.

"I'm a Texan," he said. His tone was just short of curt. "Down my way, a man expects to protect himself no matter who's around."

The Egyptian smiled.

The show began.

Eerie sounds, like voices from the grave, began to whisper all around him. The Sphinx seemed to speak. Powerful spotlights stabbed the sky.

Shaw was awed and frightened.

YAKOV KATZENELENBOGEN breathed hard as he climbed one level of cut rocks after another. Two and a half million huge stone blocks had been stacked there by slaves long dead. Katz began to feel he was climbing every stone individually.

Time and the elements had wiped away most of the ancient fill-in material that had once made the pyramids appear smooth on all sides. The stones, each more than waist high, made for slow climbing.

Katz, seeing figures above him, took a precaution against the unexpected. He took out and held the Steyr Model GB automatic pistol that he had bought from a kid after passing customs inspection at the border. He carried other weapons in addition to the gun. There was a plastic garrote in his left heel and a square of plastic explosive in the right.

Also, he wore the artificial arm with the .22-caliber straight-rod gun in the index finger and a stiletto hidden below the elbow.

As he unholstered the Steyr, a voice spoke to him from above. "Katz," it called.

The accent identified the speaker right away. It was their own trusted Rafael Encizo.

"Everybody there?" Katz whispered back.

"Everybody but our elderly leader," Calvin James kidded.

Katz climbed faster to catch up with the others. He would not let a twenty-nine-year-old outpace him.

Near the top, all five Phoenix team members soon perched cautiously, each covering a different direction.

"You got anything new on this Sadam animal?" asked Gary Manning.

"Not yet." A strong wind buffeted Katz as he looked up at the belly of a helicopter. It was flying a couple of hundred feet up, flanked by two other choppers with their lights probing shadows along approaches to the grandstands.

"The President-elect is down there," James said. "Obviously we're here to watch over him."

"They got an army of bodyguards. He probably doesn't need us," Katz said. "We're after Sadam, and the VP, unfortunately, is the bait. If this maniac Sadam does assassinate the next President of the United States, he'll be a hero to all the anti-American fanatics in the Middle East. Hell, he could probably win over every splinter group in Lebanon. Libya would swoon in his arms. Iran and the Palestinians would die for him."

"We're talking major catastrophe here, guys," said McCarter. "So it's our kind of game. Big. Rough. And no rules."

"Hey," Encizo said. "Look. It's over. The dignitaries are leaving."

"After I climbed this giant tombstone?" Katz grumbled.

While the others were watching the crowd, Manning turned his attention to an ear-beating sound.

"A chopper," he said. "Coming down on us."

Katz cocked his head. The clatter had become a roar.

"It's one of the three security choppers," James insisted.

"Coming in to pick up the big shots?" McCarter asked.

"They're in their cars already," James told him.

As if choreographed, Phoenix Force drew their weapons. No one needed to say it. A chopper could be part of an assassination attempt.

As the dark, flailing bird approached, all five members braced for battle.

Its lights pointed forward, sweeping over the Phoenix team.

The markings identified her as an old Army workhorse that had survived the Vietnam war. It was large enough to carry more than a squad of grunts and their weaponry into action.

The side door was open.

The rope that dropped nearly hit Katz on the head. He grabbed it and held on.

"It's ours," he said. "Keep me covered, just in case." He clutched the rope.

James laughed. "Keep you covered? You'll be hanging out there like a bull's-eye."

Katz grunted. Against the down draft from the blades, using his feet and working hand over hook, he started climbing.

McCarter came up behind him.

When the helicopter moved, the rope became a swing. Just hanging on became a contest.

James followed.

The three were inching up when the helicopter swung to the right and climbed out of effective range. The men on the rope were unwilling players in a game of crack the whip.

Five minutes later, the exhausted angry Katz accepted a helping hand into the ship.

He controlled his fury long enough to help McCarter and James aboard, and pick up Encizo and Manning. After all were safely in the chopper, Katz grabbed the shirtfront of the only stranger in the passenger section.

"G'day, mates," the tall, lanky Australian said with a smile. "I'm your new nanny. Anybody wet their nappies on the way up?"

James rushed forward and shoved a weapon into the cockpit. The pilot wore the uniform of a Cairo police officer. The copilot seat was empty. The Egyptian gave the Cuban an unfriendly glare and kept his attention on the crowded airspace.

"Nobody up there but the pilot," Encizo announced. The others had checked the cargo section and found no one in hiding behind the crates at the rear of the craft.

Katz turned to the Australian.

His weathered, ageless face could be forty, give or take ten years. Early forties, Katz decided, eyeing the man's lean, fit body.

He was not pretty. His eyes were too deep-set, the nose bulky and pockmarked. Too tall to stand comfortably, he settled onto a bench on one side of the Huey. The members of Phoenix Force sat opposite him. His thinning hair retained vestiges of red, and carrot-colored fuzz ran down his freckled arms. A red-gray tuft filled in the V of his shirt.

It was too dark to see the color of his eyes.

He wore a holster on his right thigh, a strange holster, designed to hold the 18-inch Calico High Tech Model 100 .22-caliber pistol. On the seat beside him lay the pistol's big brother, the M-100 carbine. Both flaunted space-age design. The 100-round magazines clipped in behind the trigger and grip. But in their original design, the rimfire .22 long rifles were not much for stopping a man.

The Aussie answered the unasked question. "They're loaded hotter than Paddy's arse," he said. "One grain more and you'd blow away your own pinkies. The bullets explode on impact. Modified for full automatic. And remember, lads, it's like a swarm of bees. Whoever gets hit will look like a colander."

He nodded toward the back of the compartment. "Brought each of you a pair and plenty of ammo."

"We'll choose our own weapons, thanks," David McCarter insisted. His mood was foul. He had not appreciated climbing a rope to reach a man he did not know.

"No problem," the Australian said. He pointed to other boxes. "Uzis, Berettas, AK-47s, grenades, anything you're likely to want. Except for Sheilas."

"What are Sheilas?" Calvin James asked.

"Girls," McCarter answered.

"Wait." Katz raised both hands for silence. "Let's get everybody briefed before we go any farther."

"Yeah," McCarter said, "what bloody fool decided to have us picked up by a chopper dangling a rope?"

"I did, sort of," Katz said.

"Why?" Encizo was curious, not critical.

"Because the chopper was supposed to be there, beaming up the desert approaches. Nobody, including a Peeping Tom, could see past those lights while we came up. So, we're aboard and nobody knows it. More important, we're tailing the Vice President's entourage—legally."

"And we watch to see if Sadam gives it a go," McCarter concluded.

"Right." Katz had to shout to be heard. "And we all know our target: Sadam?"

"Right," three of the men chorused.

"Colonel Mohammed Sadam," McCarter said. "He terrorized the Middle East for years. Now he's branching out. He killed an American citizen on one of his skyjacking jaunts. A pretty little teenager."

"He's done a lot more than that," James said. "When we take him alive and turn him over to the government, he'll spend the rest of his life playing a bird in a cage. I'd like that."

Encizo was not so confident. "First we have to get him. Nobody even knows what he looks like or what his real name is."

"That's his mystique," Manning added. "It makes his stupid followers think they're invincible, too."

"Okay," Katz interrupted. "For now, let's get someone up front with the pilot so we can watch the motorcade properly. Calvin, want the job?"

"Sure." James moved forward.

Katz took a moment to consult his memory banks for a dossier on the Australian. The Aussie came up aces in the espionage game. He was Australia's equivalent of Phoenix Force.

He had a way of doing exactly what was needed—capture, disable or kill. There was only one small problem. At home, he frequently holed up in a pub and bragged about his exploits, to the embarrassment of his superiors.

"Have you been banished for long this time, Aussie?" Katz asked.

"Long enough to smell like a camel."

Katz nodded.

"It's no easy game, you know, mate. Not Sadam's bag of jackeroos."

"I hear they're calling themselves Sadamites now," Manning said.

McCarter sneered. "It's got a religious ring to it. Nothing like a little prayer before murdering a bunch of innocent kids and folks too old to run."

Katz settled back and let himself sink into exhaustion. The rush to the pyramid had drained him. And he was worried. The team had chased down some savvy villains in its time, but Sadam was a dangerous mixture of genius and recklessness.

He had charisma, too. The media in the Muslim world tended to treat him as Hollywood treated Jesse James and Billy the Kid and Robin Hood. He was a hero.

In the States, his face would have been on baseball trading cards.

That kind of public conception was difficult to fight.

So Katz worried. Something told him not all of them would come through this mission unscathed.

5

The Huey pilot followed the vice-presidential caravan through the crowded city by watching the flashing lights of the lead cars. Like the other pilots, he kept the craft far back.

In the noisy copter, the Phoenix Force members squirmed irritably. They wanted to be down where the action might erupt.

"This is crazy, pure loco," Rafael Encizo griped. "How can anyone provide protection from so far away?"

At a window, David McCarter held one of the modified Calico High Tech .22-caliber carbines. He had taken it from the crates at the rear of the chopper and loaded a 100-round magazine. One of the special holsters with a pistol version was low on his hip.

Katz watched him uneasily. The Britisher aimed out the window, making machine gun noises like a kid.

McCarter's lust for action occasionally bothered Katz. Yet he always followed the code. He never killed except when the mission required.

Manning was equally irritable. "Tell the pilot to put us down," he told Katz. "We're not accomplishing anything up here."

"Yeah, I'm for putting this mother down and having at least some of us on the ground," said Encizo.

They were not telling Katz what to do, just expressing their own viewpoints. For all they knew, Katz might be under orders to stay aloft. They had not asked.

And with Colonel Sadam on the loose, they feared for the Vice President. They had not been sent after such an internationally known target in months. They wanted to be down where they could actively protect the VP.

The Australian said, "You want to land? Point to a place and I'll have you bushrangers on the ground in five minutes."

Katz gave him a withering look. "Hold the course," the Israeli said.

He was not deaf to the others' concerns. To double-check his decision, Katz went up front to replace Calvin James.

"Nothing unusual so far," the black American said as he gave up his seat.

Sitting down, Katz craned his neck to see the string of official cars move through a brightly lit section of a broad boulevard.

The pilot beside him was an Arab who spoke no English, but the engine noise made it nearly impossible for Katz to communicate verbally anyway.

VICE PRESIDENT STEPHEN SHAW pretended interest as the vehicle stopped in front of the infamous reviewing stand.

"Anwar al-Sadat died here," the Egyptian leader said softly.

He was referring to the man who had once been a terrorist who had fought the king that the English had imposed on the country, and the whole British Colonial army. He had died a hero, victim of a few disloyal army troops.

A head of state was fair game anywhere in the world, Shaw knew all too well.

He remembered something the current American President had told him after the election that made Shaw his successor.

"You'll have a platoon of security men and police and FBI agents surrounding you at all times when you travel beyond the White House to talk to the people who elected us."

"You're telling me I'll be safe?" Shaw had said.

"No," the older politician said with a smile. "I'm telling you to keep in practice with that Beretta of yours."

Remembering, Shaw sat with his hand inside his suit as the caravan slowed again.

The neighborhood was not reassuring. It was the counterpart of any American slum where gangs shot out the streetlights as fast as they are replaced. Graffiti disfigured the long wall on the right. While most of it was unintelligible, Shaw read the English words, Kill the American bastards. Allah has spoken.

"Pay no attention," the Egyptian president said. "I gave orders to have all such insults painted over. Apparently my men missed a few."

Running along the wall was a foot-deep pile of papers and refuse. To the left, bare twenty-five-watt bulbs illuminated the food and souvenir stands. Shoppers pressed close to the official vehicle. The few who dared to touch the vehicle were roughed up. Several stands were overturned and their produce squashed under the tires of cars and motorcycles.

The motorcycle escort turned through a gate and the armored car followed. A dirt road replaced the potholed pavement of the past few miles.

Without warning the armored car stopped and the driver jumped out.

Stephen Shaw watched as his own man attempted to grab the driver, saying, "Wait. What is this?"

The president of Egypt turned to Shaw as the driver opened the door on his side.

"Preserving skeletons and rotted flesh are against my religion," the official said. "I will leave you to pay your respects to your ancestors."

Shaw echoed his bodyguard. "Wait."

Before he could decide whether he should follow his host, the choice was no longer his. Another driver slid behind the wheel. The car rolled forward again.

The premonition washed in like the surf. Sweat glistened on Shaw's cheeks. His hands felt slick. His face was hot, his mouth dry.

Secret Service people were trotting alongside the armored vehicle.

Lights lined the narrow driveway, blinding him.

They made the City of the Dead even more ominous. It was like a scene in a horror movie. All that was missing was the eerie background music.

The mausoleums were strongly built and decorated with bronze flowers and religious figurines. Each structure was at least as large as a garage, many the size of a modest home. Marble facades and grand pillars made the tombs resemble miniature palaces from the days of the pharaohs. Several had two-story statues of pharaohs or gods beside their heavy bronze doors.

Streets just wide enough for a car divided the city into blocks. In places the crumbling of the stone walls made the streets even narrower, so that only a horse and cart could pass.

"Families try to build better tombs than their neighbors," the Egyptian driver said, to Shaw's surprise. The Vice President had not expected the driver to know English, or how to use the intercom between the driver's and the passenger compartments of the vehicle.

He breathed easier, though, seeing that his bodyguard held his weapon in his lap, the muzzle casually pointed at the back of the driver.

"Some look thousands of years old," Shaw remarked.

"They are. When people die, they are buried on top of their ancestors. It is the way."

Shaw slowly looked about him. The conical areas beneath the temporary lighting standards made it seem as though he were in a child-sized city. He relaxed. There were many men to protect him.

At the edge of the illuminated area, the crypts were in stately shadows. The huge stone guardians seemed to frown on this invasion of their privacy. From far away, the glow of Cairo created grotesque, misshapen gargoyles on their roofs, and shadows that moved like ghosts among the stone houses.

"All right," Shaw said into the intercom. "I've seen it. Let's pick up the president and get on to the banquet."

His bodyguard said, "One moment, sir."

Two Americans approached the vehicle. Shaw recognized Leonard Toby, the man in charge of protocol, and Major Allen Lukes in full uniform.

The Vice President rolled down the window. "Get me out of here," he told them. "Get me the hell out of here."

"In a moment, sir," Toby said.

"Now."

The major said, "I'll get up to the lead motorcycle and try to get us moving." He disappeared from the lighted area.

Meanwhile, Toby reached in to open the door. "Sir, it will take a moment for the major to get to the front of the column. So you might as well get out and pay homage to your ancestors."

"Damn."

The door was open.

"Yours was a rich and powerful family once. Some Egyptians might be insulted if you don't visit your family tomb."

"I don't give a damn about family tombs." But Shaw already had one foot out of the car, and Secret Service men were forming a wall with their bodies.

Toby pointed to a work of art, a stone mausoleum with ancient-looking figures towering beside the doors. It was among the most spectacular of the tombs.

"Damn," Shaw said.

He reassured himself by touching the Beretta before he exited. Dozens of guards were all around.

He had not needed all of these people in Nam. Why did he need them here?

Then he was outside in the hot, humid night. He felt bathed in his own sweat. A light shone on the large tomb, which resembled the Parthenon.

His driver pointed to words in Arabic over the open bronze door. "Your name," the man said.

Shaw felt his throat constricting.

"Go," the driver urged. "Inside. Please."

"No."

"We checked the place, sir," a Secret Service man said. "It's completely safe. But you don't have to go inside. These places always look kind of scary."

Was the man suggesting he was afraid? Shaw asked himself. He was not afraid of anything.

Taking the flashlight handed to him, he went inside. He shone the beam on the walls. They were filled with writing and drawings in a style fashionable a thousand years ago.

He stumbled and fell flat across a slab of concrete. Rising, he swept the light around the floor. There were at least six concrete slabs marked with the names of people buried below. There was room for more names.

God. Have they left space for me? Already?

He forced himself to be casual as he exited. He felt chilled in the stifling night.

"Are you all right, sir?"

"Yes. I've paid my respects. Now let's get out of here."

The sounds stopped him.

The worst came from the helicopters that hovered above him. Their beams turned downward like mobile stage lights.

The security people made him feel better. The cowardice seeped away.

It was just a cemetery.

A figure sprinted across the street at the edge of the light, and Shaw pointed and said excitedly, "Hey! I saw somebody run between the buildings."

He turned back to the car.

"It's all right, sir," his bodyguard told him. "A few people live in here."

"Living people?"

"They have nowhere else. Most of them are from wealthy families that have fallen on hard times. No one stops them from living in the family crypt."

A child peered around another building.

Shaw vowed to himself to do something to help these people when he moved into the White House.

He felt safer.

Until the lights went out.

6

When the floodlights went out in the City of the Dead, Katz tensed for action, his body a coiled spring of muscle.

From the Huey helicopter, which hovered in front of the other official aircraft, it was plain to see that the mosaic below had changed distinctly.

One moment a row of lights glowed in the dead black of the expansive cemetery. An instant later, the brightest lights had blinked out, leaving only the headlights of the cars and motorcycles in the motorcade that had accompanied the American Vice President into the morbid tourist attraction.

Almost instinctively, Katz reviewed the bank of contingency plans he had concocted while en route from Israel. He settled on the plan he had developed for an assassination attempt in the city of darkness.

"Take us down—fast!" he yelled in the Arabic he had picked up in bits and pieces during his frequent sojourns in the Middle East. "Something is wrong down there."

The pilot stared at him. He had understood, but he said he took orders only from his superior, the Australian.

Headlights began going out on the vehicles below. Figures crouched behind cars.

"Down!" the senior Phoenix Force member commanded again. He was ready to use his weapon as a threat as the Australian poked his head into the compartment.

"Tell the pilot to put us down. As close as he can get to the headlights. Now."

The Arab shook his head. He had no intention of landing in a patchwork of roofs and narrow roads.

For Aussie, Katz aimed the hook of his prosthetic arm at the mere pinpoints of light left inside the morbid city.

The Australian laughed. "Not for all the johnny-cakes in 'stralia."

Katz reached forward and held the Aussie's arm in a very steely grip with his prosthetic device.

He looked penetratingly long and hard at the man until a red flush suffused the Australian's face. He tried to look away but was compelled by the unflinching and commanding gaze.

"Tell him," Katz said quietly, but there was no mistaking the threat in his voice. There was no question who was more determined and in command.

The Aussie conferred briefly with the pilot, then shook Katz's steel hand away. He looked somewhat sheepish, and also a little disgusted with himself.

"He's landing us then?" Katz said.

"We're going down the way you came up."

"What's with this 'we' stuff?"

"I got orders to help you bleeding dingoes, whoever you are. And I'm tagging along like an aborigine's dog until I get told otherwise by someone bigger than you, Captain Hook."

Katz started to grab him by the throat, but he felt something press at his stomach.

Knife in hand, Aussie smiled pleasantly. He kept the knife there. "The pilot says there's no place to land and he's not going to hover so close that some Arab gunnie gets a good shot at him. So we're going down by rope, in the bloody dark."

Katz pushed past him. "Then do it. We'll break out the guns." As he passed, he glowered at the man, but in the rear compartment he smiled. He liked Aussie. He would take him with the team as long as he was useful on the mission.

Katz peered again at the ground through the small window. Something sure as hell was going down in the city of corpses.

"What's happening, chief?" Gary Manning asked for the rest.

"The floodlights went out," their leader called as he pushed back the cargo hatch and tossed the rope over the side. "Somebody is shooting out the headlights. The people on the ground don't know where to hide."

"You think it's Sadam's men?" asked McCarter, frantic with excitement. He tried to be first onto the rope.

"Do you?" Encizo asked. "Think it's Sadam?"

"Our mission has begun," Katz said. "That's all I know."

All hell was about to break loose. He could sense it.

NAHIB KAMAL, lieutenant to the mysterious Mohammed Sadam, stood behind the stand selling onions to an old woman stooped from years of poverty.

His attention left her as he collected the money. The stands in either direction were crowded with impatient customers. The shopkeepers fretted, trying to complete one sale so they could move on to the next.

The next sale would never come.

Kamal had seen the lights flick off in the cemetery. His people had cut the cable the government provided into the dead city.

He saw one of the younger Sadamites—as their troops were called—raise his hand down the street.

Good. The electricity would not come on again. The temporary cables had been sufficiently cut and scrambled.

Kamal could hear the muffled shots and the sound of exploding headlights from inside the city. Excellent.

Everything was on schedule.

Now if he could only make certain that his men wouldn't panic in the bedlam that would come. If they killed the wrong man, all would be for nothing.

Be calm, Kamal told himself. Send in the next wave.

He turned and nodded at a man shopping at a trinket shop forty yards away.

The entire marketplace erupted into activity.

Men, women, children turned away from the stands. The young men in Western dress were the first through the gates and over the wall. The children were next. Some were allowed to get in front of the men, decoys that hopefully would confuse the security men around the Vice President of the United States.

The women, all older, wore widows' black. Many could no more than waddle. They were ghostly figures as they passed by Kamal and blended into the darkness.

He smiled. "What a few piasters will buy," he said aloud.

His men had spent the past hour distributing coins to anyone "brave enough" to run through the City of the Dead after dark. They gave no explanations, moving too fast to be remembered.

Those who agreed—and virtually everyone had done so—were paid immediately and given the promise of more on the far side. Avarice fostered secrecy. Those chosen feared there would be too many runners and too little money at the end.

The guards stationed at the entrances were overwhelmed as young boys jumped on their backs and wrestled them to the ground. Not a shot was fired. Weapons were wrested from hands of men who hesitated to kill children.

The security forces inside the city, still stunned by the power failure, were unaware that hundreds of people were converging upon them. They turned from one vehicle to another as headlights exploded. It was a scenario that no agency had foreseen.

The Vice President reacted immediately—he drew his Beretta.

He stunned everyone around him, until the young protocol officer Leonard Toby leaped forward and wrestled it away.

"For Christ's sake, sir, this isn't Texas."

Shaw's personal bodyguard rushed in to retrieve his superior's weapon. He stopped a yard short, his expression one of bafflement. He put his hand over his shoulder as if a bug had crawled under his shirt.

His eyes rolled back and he collapsed quietly in the dirt.

"My God!" The Vice President swung around, reaching for his weapon.

"Sir, please," Toby shouted. "If anybody sees you with this, they may shoot before they recognize you."

"He's right." Major Allen Lukes appeared from the dark.

"In the car, sir. We'll have it moving in a minute."

Shaw's premonition had come true, but his courage returned. He considered his position in light of the national interest. He was not just the Vice President any longer. He was the President-elect. If anything happened to him before the inauguration, the political hack who had run with him would step into the White House. Although the man was a vote getter, his only credentials were his charisma and his family name. He was volatile enough to offend one of the superpowers into a nuclear confrontation.

I have to live, Shaw decided.

He entered the car, closed the door and sat erect. He would not cower. He would trust the bulletproof glass.

Outside, automatic fire streaked through the night. One after another, headlights blinked out. Shaw saw a mausoleum door open and a man appear, holding a 9 mm assault carbine.

Hadn't his men gone from vault to vault making sure they were locked on the outside?

Yet another door opened. Another gunman started firing from within.

An Egyptian security man swung an M-16 toward the open door. The long burst he fired streaked toward the dark sky as he absorbed a belly full of lead.

The front door of the limousine opened and a cleancut young man peered into the rear compartment. He rapped on the glass that separated the front seat from the rear. When the Vice President hesitated, the young man held his Secret Service credentials to the glass. Shaw lowered the glass.

The man smiled. "Good evening, sir." He raised an unusually designed hand gun. It popped and something from its muzzle stung the Vice President's shoulder.

Shaw slipped into a swirling, milky pit, and everything became soft and silent.

THE MEMBERS OF PHOENIX FORCE had brief, bird's-eye views as they slid down the rope. Their hands burned, sacrificed to the need for haste.

In the chaotic darkness it was impossible to decipher what was happening. Dark figures were running throughout the cemetery, converging on the few remaining vehicle lights at the center of "town." Guns spit deadly jets of flame.

The government helicopter pilots dropped low, turning on their powerful beams. Immediately, as if hungering for new prey, streams of tracers honed in. The lights of one chopper shattered and went out. The pilot hauled his craft up and away. Another, its lights still intact, tilted like a bird with a broken wing. Then it hit the ground near the city and burst into bright flames.

The pilot for Phoenix Force steadied his chopper as the team members dropped from the rope. Katz was the last man out.

From the end of the rope, Katz looked down. It was a long drop. The pilot had misjudged.

"Gotta stop this sort of thing someday," he said aloud. "Old bones break easy."

He dropped.

One foot landed neatly on a level roof, the other missed. He fell an extra twelve feet. Calvin James broke his fall, trying to catch the leader in his arms. They both ended up bruised and battered.

"You okay?" James asked, though he was somewhat pre-occupied as he checked out his own scraped and bleeding shoulder.

"I'm bruised from head to foot. Some bastard got between me and the soft ground."

"You ungrateful..."

Katz slapped him on the shoulder. "All right, you get the Bronze Star for damned foolishness. You could have put the two of us out of commission."

Despite the limp he could not hide, he managed to keep up with the others. Most of his life had been lived at full speed, sprinting toward action and danger. If he backed away from a dangerous situation, he did it only to find a better angle of attack.

Occasionally Katz thought he courted death because he had lost his craving for life after his wife died.

But he'd been fighting as a teenager even before he met her. Always a booster of a free Israel, he still returned to his spiritual home to defend it against constant terrorist attacks, but he fought for other causes, too.

Tonight he was rushing to assist the American Vice President. His assigned target was Mohammed Sadam. He doubted he would see the sadistic killer, but was certain to see the Sadamites, who made up the attacking force. On the ground, he might get a line on Sadam. At the very least, he would thin the ranks of his followers.

As soon as Katz and the others had dropped from the helicopter rope, they began to chase the shadowy figures darting past, who appeared to be non-combatants.

Katz knocked an old woman to the ground as he rounded one of the mansionlike structures. He had to put his carbine down as he helped her to her feet. Apologizing, he nearly lost his rifle to a boy no more than eight years old.

He snared the boy by the arm. "What's going on?" he asked in Arabic. "Why are all the people running through the cemetery?"

"Fire," the boy lied. "A terrible fire."

Having fallen behind during this exchange, Katz was trying to get ahead when he heard the first shots. Instinctively he flung himself to the ground. The others found cover behind miniature marble palaces. All except Aussie. He stood in the middle of the narrow road and laughed.

"They're shooting in the other direction," he taunted. "You kiddies can get up now."

"Oh, yeah?" Katz scoffed.

A moment later, a rain of bullets splashed dust in a line headed straight for Aussie's feet. He danced as Gary Manning found the source of the automatic blast. Going full auto with the carbine, Manning triggered out twenty rounds.

The gunman twisted and turned as practically every slug poked a small-caliber hole into his head and upper torso. Eventually he dropped his weapon and covered his face with his hands. He went down on his knees, then fell forward into the dirt.

"Hell," McCarter said, "he could be one of the good guys."

The thought spread through the team.

In the dark and mad chaos there was no telling a legal kill from a murder.

"Sadam," Gary Manning said. "This has to be his doing."

Even as he spoke, women continued to run past, as did men in Western dress, some with guns. In most cases the moonlight left that open to question.

"Yeah, Sadam," Katz agreed.

It was the kind of lavish scheme the flamboyant revolutionary was noted for. He hijacked airports, not just single aircraft. He did not car-bomb Jewish ambassadors in London, he tried to topple the Eiffel Tower. Ten months back he had taken credit for the deadly destruction of an American spacecraft seconds after its launch.

"He's after the Vice President," Rafael Encizo shouted.

No one disagreed. Momentarily, they felt stymied and helpless. If they charged into the melee near the stalled motorcade, they would not know whom to attack.

As nearly as Katz could tell, the security forces of both countries were fighting a common foe. Little fire came from the hub of the struggle. The shooting came from the surrounding buildings.

Katz gambled. If he made the wrong decision, he might take the other guys with him. But his military genius told him to set parameters.

"Hit the guys inside the tombs," he shouted over the hubbub. "Avoid everybody else if you can."

His teammates, even the Australian, did not hesitate. They rose and started running, trying to ignore the bullets hissing at them from the legitimate security men in the center.

Only those inside the tombs, the Sadamites, were fair game.

Reaching one stone structure, whose door was open a scant two inches, Katz dropped to his knees, jammed his pistol through the crack and fired.

An unseen target cried out. He could be heard stumbling about on the marble. Finally he fell and was quiet.

McCarter had a different technique. Casually, so as not to attract attention from the dying guards, he slid along a wall, snatched a protruding AK-47 and yanked outward. A startled scarecrow of a man stumbled out, unable to release his weapon fast enough.

McCarter tripped him, then pinned his neck and face to the ground. He put the carbine to the back of the man's head.

"*Ma el-selama,* kid," McCarter said.

He used one shot.

Almost no blood exited the wound. Drops made a little puddle that was quickly absorbed by the dry dirt of the road.

Gary Manning also tried the casual approach. Striding between the milling women and kids who were now thinning out, he passed within five yards of the remaining security guards. None of them could figure him out. Besides, they were too busy trying to hide. At the nearest bronze door where an MP-83 automatic look-alike poked out, the Canadian rapped with the butt of his own weapon. A face tentatively peeped out.

Enemies didn't knock, the terrorist must have figured.

Manning blew away the face and walked on, looking for new targets.

Calvin tried Manning's knock-knock game and got pulled inside. In the pitch-darkness, he and his enemy had trapped each other.

Fire first and live, if your first shot was a kill. Fire first and miss... you'd be sausage.

The tomb smelled musty. It seemed to magnify every sound, especially to his taut nerves. He could almost swear that heavy breathing reverberated in every corner. But where did it come from? All he was sure of was that he wasn't alone. Move and stumble. Stumble and die.

Something flew and slammed against a wall. James almost fired at the decoy. He wanted to laugh, to jeer at the man who shared this magnificent coffin.

I didn't fall for that one, sucker, the black American congratulated himself.

Then he sat down quietly. He took off a shoe and stripped it of laces. Next he tied a slipknot around his pistol's trigger and guard. He tied the other end of the laces around his ankle. When he jerked his foot, the pistol fired.

Instantly, bullets zipped at the pistol.

Immediately Calvin James swung the carbine toward the muzzle-flash and hailed the area with .22 zingers.

When the unseen enemy fell, James had to hunt for his shoe.

Outside the battle was abating. All the unarmed decoys were gone; the surviving security guards were dropping their weapons and attempting to escape in cars or motorcycles or on their feet.

Sirens sounding from every direction were closing in on the cemetery.

One of the vehicles, an armored Cadillac, was picking up speed.

"That's Shaw's car," Katz called.

He and Encizo had a chance of grabbing a door handle or maybe the bumper, but a burly Secret Service man appeared at the rear.

The big man's gun pointed at McCarter's head, but Katz broke the guard's ankle with his carbine. The big guy dropped his gun and cried in pain.

Katz saw Manning and McCarter start after the Cadillac.

In the dying turmoil, Leonard Toby, the American protocol officer, stood alone in the intersection where the battle had centered.

"They've got the Vice President," Toby yelled. "They've got Shaw."

Katz saw him and remembered him from somewhere.

The Israeli nearly went after the VP, but the helicopters were returning. The flashing lights of police vehicles were approaching the far entrance.

It looked as if he was trapped with bodies all around and no plausible alibi.

But there was Aussie. He stood alone on top of the tallest mausoleum and motioned toward their old Huey.

Katz clambered up the rope while police yapped below like frustrated hounds.

"Keep up the good work, lads," he needled as the copter moved away. "Maybe next time you'll arrive in time for the party."

7

Gary Manning pulled a dead Cairo police officer from his motorcycle and jumped into the saddle. Despite the headlight knocked out by gunfire, he roared through the dark cemetery. Seconds later, seeing an iron grillwork loom ahead, he wrenched the machine into a ninety-degree turn and stopped parallel to the barrier.

The gate had been jammed behind the escaping car. The opening was only wide enough for pedestrians, and he was forced to dismount to get the handlebars through.

He was moments ahead of McCarter and Encizo.

An uneven dirt street led off to the right and left. Another route, better maintained, extended straight ahead. Manning took that course. McCarter and Encizo split to search in other directions.

The Canadian roared ahead. It was not like driving on the open roads of the bush country of Manning's native Canada. It was worse than a Toronto traffic jam.

Spurred by curiosity, the entire neighborhood stampeded toward the action. Now that the war was over, everybody wanted to see the carnage.

Manning put on the siren. He yelled, "Out of the way. Police. Give me room."

Then he remembered, few of the people would understand English.

He rode with his feet off the rests, using them to keep his balance when he was forced to slow to a pedestrian speed. His only hope was that the Vice President's car was also crawling through a mob.

After two blocks, he spotted the Cadillac and switched to new tactics. Taking the pistol from its oversize holster, he began firing in the air.

With bullets buzzing over the tallest heads, he garnered respect. Nothing stood between him and the escaping car. He was catching up fast when one of the vehicle's windows rolled down and a belch of flame spit back at him.

He left a six-inch skid on the pavement as he turned suddenly to avoid getting hit. He worked the carbine free while still moving. He picked one rear wheel of the Cadillac and pumped nearly forty rounds into the reinforced rubber. The tire finally blew, and the driver lost control.

Immediately six men left the car.

Three blasted the street around Manning while two more pushed a man in a business suit ahead of them. His hands were behind his back as if he were cuffed or tied. He shuffled and stumbled as his apparent captors shoved him up the street.

They were short, dressed in trousers and short-sleeved shirts.

"Sadam's men," the Canadian assured himself.

He aimed at the man on the far right and squeezed off a short burst. A second burst caught the man in the buttocks. He dropped his grip on his prisoner. Manning swept his weapon to his left.

He did not get a shot off.

The threesome who were not occupied with the prisoner walked steadily up the street, laying down a field of marching fire.

Manning rested his rifle on the motorcycle's fuel tank and got off one killing shot before the rifle clicked.

He had used all one hundred bullets.

He yanked the odd-shaped pistol into action, but he could not count on the accuracy he got with the carbine.

Then the enemy changed tactics. They aimed at the motorcycle's fuel tank. Bullets cracked beside Manning's head or nipped his shoulders. As he rolled and moved to make himself a difficult target, the kidnappers were getting closer and closer.

He felt he was going to die.

And they kept approaching.

Their leader, one of Nahib Kamal's sergeants, grinned with pleasure. He had lost half his crew in the gunfight. Kamal might kill him for not protecting his men adequately, but for a moment, he was triumphant. He and his men were going to kill one of the fearless animals that had dropped from a helicopter to disrupt the entire mission.

"You!" He pointed to one of his men. "To the right. Keep shooting. Don't give him a chance to raise his head."

Manning recognized the problem. They were closing fast, but moving from cover to cover.

"You," the sergeant said to the man on his left. "Faster. A quick kill and we leave."

Manning could not understand the orders, but he knew his position was no longer defendable. He had two choices. Stay and burn when the tank blew, or run and die with a bullet in the back.

In a desperate switch of tactics, he combined the choices. As the Sadamites stopped for more accurate shots, he suddenly rolled back from the bike's shield, and shot into the gas tank.

It exploded into a yellow and red ball of fire. The heat set his shirt on fire, but he squelched that with one roll.

The rolling had put him in the open, but the fire made him invisible. Each of Sadam's men raised an arm to shade his eyes.

Gary Manning rolled farther to the side. He caught the enemy with all their attention on the fire.

Manning squeezed the trigger.

Only one of them escaped, and he rushed in the direction that the VP had been taken. On his way, he checked the man who had caught a six-pack of .22s in the ass. He was still alive—until his partner blew away the side of his face.

A tough bunch. They took prisoners but did not leave wounded to be questioned.

Manning rose, becoming aware of a sticky warmth draining down his forehead. Still, he ran after the kidnappers. He entered a street of small shops, all protected with heavy steel grating. He saw the taillights of a car speeding blocks away. Frustrated, he tried doors and grates. All were locked.

Police sirens approaching put an end to the chase. If they saw him with his guns, they would take after him.

Looking back, though, he was certain the cops had not seen him. They seemed intent on the corpses he had left in the street and the armor-clad Cadillac.

Spectators were pointing in the direction the survivors and their captive had taken. Manning was on the same street the kidnappers had used. He could not continue his search. It was fruitless, anyway. The men who took the VP were long gone.

He walked to another street.

For the first time in half an hour, the Canadian began checking the damage to his body. He was scraped, bruised and wounded.

And alive.

But he had failed to stop the abductors. So had the other Phoenix Team members. Nor had they hit their prime target, Mohammed Sadam.

As he felt himself about to slump into depression, the old Huey hovered above him. He expected to climb the rope again, but the copter descended to a vacant lot. Manning saw Aussie first. But behind him were the others.

When the Canadian boarded, Katz got out.

"Hey, where are you going?"

"He's going back to the cemetery," Aussie told him.

"But what about the Vice President?"

"We've lost track of him," McCarter said calmly. "We're going to regroup before we make another move. Katz thinks he can get a lead back where he's going."

The chopper climbed fast and was gone before Katz joined the growing number of spectators still piling in to see the carnage.

He reached the second row of curiosity seekers to find that only two Americans were unscathed. One was an Army major. He appeared to be stunned as he told investigators his name was Allen Lukes, personal aide to the missing VP.

The second American, Katz had met somewhere before.

"Leonard Toby, protocol officer at the embassy," Toby told an officer.

Bull! You're CIA, Katz thought, remembering. Toby was a roving agent, practically without restrictions. He had wandered the Middle East for several years, building a name for himself inside espionage and covert action circles.

"I felt a needle poke me. I was dazed before the shooting started. I did what I could. There was one strange thing. Five or six men descended from a helicopter."

"You think they kidnapped your Vice President?"

"No. They killed a lot of the terrorists."

"Would you recognize them now?"

"No. But one had a prosthetic device in place of his right hand."

"Prosthetic?" The investigating officer looked confused.

"He had a hook in place of his hand."

"Ah," said the detective. "He should be easy to trace."

Katz slipped back into the crowd. He eased his way out of the cemetery and began taking one taxi after another until he was within walking distance of the Hyatt Hotel. From there he walked as if he were tacking a sailboat.

No one followed him, of that he was certain. His arm, though, could attract unwanted attention, especially if the local police put out an all-points bulletin on a one-armed man.

He rode the service elevator to the floor where Hal Brognola had rented rooms for his team. Inside, the Australian was sleeping on the couch until he heard the door.

"Well, g'day, mate, glad to have you back from the bush."

Manning paced. McCarter sat on the floor, field-stripping his weapons. Encizo turned from the window, and Calvin James emerged from the bathroom, his cheeks coated with shaving cream.

"Where've you been?" McCarter said irritably.

"We were about to send out a patrol for you," said Manning.

Encizo said, "Brognola called from the Farm. He thinks we're on Sadam's trail."

"We are." Katz dropped into an easy chair.

"You think that was a Sadam caper?" said James.

McCarter fitted the pieces of his carbine back together. "Nobody else would put a platoon of fanatics in vaults and think to cover the action with maybe a hundred or more decoys. Besides, he's in town."

Katz ignored the jabber. He spoke directly to the Australian. "You're supposed to be our gofer, right?"

Aussie launched into a short poem. "I will eat your Norfolk dumpling, like a juicy Spanish plum. Even dance the Newgate hornpipe, if you'll only gimme rum!"

"I need another prosthetic device, one that looks like a real hand. Got to have it fast."

"It awaits you in your boudoir. Anything else? Like new guns, perhaps?"

"Yeah, everybody is going to ID us if we use the hundred-shot plinkers again."

"Everything's cheerio. You'll find new toys for the boys in your suitcases. Anything else?"

"Yeah, like where Sadam is right now?"

"In Cairo yet, I should say."

"Big help," McCarter grumbled. "Real big help."

8

Nahib Kamal found himself immobilized.

The excitement in the cemetery had drawn all the shoppers to the area. Only the street merchants did not leave their stalls, for fear of losing their wares.

Kamal scorned their poverty. The fools did not have funds to buy new inventory. They lived their lives chained to their stalls. While Cairo was not a city of starving people, many lived at a subsistence level from day to day.

Kamal had a fortune in banks throughout Europe. One day he planned to retire and buy a home on an island in the Nile. First, though, he had a hunger as gnawing as starvation. He wanted to rule the Sadamites. After Sadam had retired, of course. Or died. Or was imprisoned.

Stop, he told himself. Such thoughts could be read by men like Sadam.

He jerked himself back to reality.

Residents of the bleak apartment buildings surrounding the City of the Dead flocked into the war zone. Nothing aroused such interest as death. Only a public execution could have presented a stronger attraction.

The arrival of the police with their harsh lights and urgent sirens added to the sport. While the officers tried to cordon off the gate, interlopers climbed over the walls.

Fearful of making himself suspect, Kamal shouted questions at people who came out.

"What is going on in there?" he called.

"There are dead bodies. Many dead bodies," answered one youth.

"How many?"

"No one knows," he said, and retched in the street.

Kamal asked another sightseer who had been killed.

"The President of the United States and all his guards."

"Vice President," Kamal corrected him. He felt weak with fear. Surely the fools who served under him had not killed the American politician. If they had, he, Kamal, would have to flee for his life. Sadam would never tolerate such incompetence.

He questioned others.

"How many were killed?"

"Enough to fill a second City of the Dead."

"Were all those dead dressed in suits?"

"By no means."

That meant some of his own men were dead.

He could always recruit more human fodder. He had a flair for enticing young men with stories of the great Colonel Mohammed Sadam, a man of mystery, a man who would lead the entire Arab world one day. Those who followed him now would help him rule.

Legions of men in Lebanon and Yemen were waiting to fight alongside Colonel Mohammed Sadam.

So the great man's lieutenant was unprepared to see Colonel Sadam appear from inside the cemetery.

Kamal marveled at the colonel's audacity. He wore no scarf across his face. No dyed hair. No makeup.

The man could do that. Only his one lieutenant knew his real identity.

"Such nice fruit you have," Sadam said for the benefit of the other shopkeepers.

"Thank you."

"Do you have tea?"

"Inside, yes." Kamal's heartbeat echoed in his chest. His leader was being reckless by allowing them to be seen together even in this pigsty that passed as a street.

"May I come in, then? I am exhausted."

"Of course." Kamal's knees threatened to give out as he led the way into the hovel behind the stand. With trembling hands he poured tea from a coffee can. "Well?" he said impatiently.

Had the mission failed? Was the intended captive dead by mistake? Had he, Kamal, failed? Was Sadam here to exact retribution?

In the name of God, why didn't Sadam speak?

"We have him," Sadam said.

His lieutenant tried to hide his relief. "I heard he was dead."

"Everything went as planned. Our people took the car with the decoy in it. Three of them are dead."

"Small loss."

Colonel Sadam's ice-blue eyes froze on his subordinate. Apparently the great man did not like indifference shown regarding his dead soldiers.

Quickly Kamal explained. "I am so relieved that you survived, that I have little pity left for the others."

Sadam's glare softened. "You don't know how few of ours survived."

"How many?"

The self-proclaimed colonel began calculating. "The decoy and two others." He paused. "Three more who escaped in the chaos."

Kamal raised his voice. "Only six are still alive? I cannot believe it."

"There were two wounded that could not be left behind."

"You found that difficult?" Kamal sought the answer so that he could better understand the man to whom he had tied his life.

Sadam ignored the question. "Our people wiped out the Secret Service men and the other bodyguards. Everyone was killed or wounded."

"But you lived. Allah speaks."

Sadam laughed.

"The other man we wished to save?"

"He survived, too."

Kamal sipped at the tea. "If our people wiped out the bodyguards, how did it come to pass that so many of ours are dead?"

"There were demons. From the sky."

"I do not understand."

Colonel Sadam was slow to answer. "I saw everything. A helicopter put down five or six men."

"Egyptian or American?"

"Neither."

"Neither?"

"Yes. That is the strange part. They certainly were not in uniform, nor were they in suits and ties. But they quickly discovered our men as they came out of their positions. The men from the helicopter killed like professionals."

"Describe them."

"Describe men I saw for an instant in the heat of battle? Impossible. But one had a hook for a right arm."

"A hook?" Kamal leaned forward. He had a nugget of information that might restore his image in Sadam's eyes.

"Yes?"

"I know of such a person." Kamal relaxed. He had his superior's interest. Perhaps Sadam would not blame him for the heavy losses. "I have heard about such a man—Jewish, I believe—who has killed many people in spite of his handicap."

Sadam's face, with no turban pulled down over his forehead or scarf covering to the bridge of his nose, betrayed the leader. Apparently he had heard of such a man, too.

Kamal had generally fought against soldiers, police, men and women hostages. They competed within restraints of law that he was not obliged to obey.

The man with the hook, however, appeared to represent no one. So the stories went, at least.

"Is he dangerous?" Sadam asked.

"Yes. Very."

"How do you know it is the same man?"

"How many such men can there be who fight with one arm?"

Kamal stood up. He was ending the conversation. It was impolite, but he wanted to leave these dangerous surroundings. The one-armed man might have seen his superior enter the hut.

"I will close the stand as soon as you leave, Colonel. I will spend what time I have avoiding the man with one arm until we are safely out of Cairo. I suggest you do the same."

Sadam rose. "We cannot bring in more men from Yemen in time, you know."

"Yes, I know."

"Then you may proceed."

Kamal smiled. Sadam always depended upon him. The wrong man was colonel. "I will do it with careful attention to each detail. Our success is predetermined."

"I expect nothing less."

9

The bold, banner-sized headlines blackened newspapers around the world.

U.S. Vice President Kidnapped.

Pedestrians halted, read the lead paragraph and fished in their pockets for the coins that would unlock the sidewalk vending machines.

In large cities, newsboys resurrected an old practice and shouted just enough of the banner to entice rushing commuters to buy the news.

Radio stations broke off the golden oldies with brief silences before DJs read from scrolling monitors fed by the international press services.

"Reliable sources have now confirmed that Vice President Stephen Shaw has been kidnapped in Cairo, Egypt, by unknown fanatics." Again a moment of silence held back the music. "I'm going to repeat that," the DJs said, uneasy in their unexpected role of newscaster. "We have just received reports that President elect Stephen Shaw has been kidnapped in Egypt by a band of gunmen... that's what it says here. Gunmen. I suppose that means terrorists."

Television stations simultaneously brought the news into virtually every home in the nation.

"President-elect Stephen Shaw has been abducted by unknown kidnappers in Cairo, Egypt," reported one anchorman. "Reports are sketchy at this moment, but the kidnapping has been confirmed. The Vice President is missing. Apparently a number of Secret Service personnel along with Egyptian security forces have been killed or wounded. The first pictures are now coming in via satellite from Cairo."

The screen filled with images of tattered bodies lying among the tombs and the curious crowd. An Egyptian police officer was shown beating a kid who clutched wallets with both hands. Blood streaking his face, the boy broke away and ran off with the booty he had taken from the newly dead.

"I'm sorry," the anchorman apologized. "Had we known the nature of those pictures, we would have advised parents to use their discretion in allowing children to watch TV at this time. Oh, and here's a notice from the White House asking for the nation to remain calm. Our staff in Washington is headed for the White House at this moment to get the latest update. For the present, though, we can say the Vice President has been reported missing in Cairo, Egypt, following a gun battle apparently involving terrorist and security forces."

In the War Room at Stony Man Farm, Hal Brognola jumped up so quickly that his high-backed swivel chair toppled to the floor. Three television screens assaulted him with the news.

His three telephones began ringing simultaneously. He picked up the red one and switched the others to hold.

The President of the United States barked his name over the phone.

"Yes, Mr. President." A chorus of voices joined Brognola's.

The Phoenix Force chief shivered. Christ! Was the chief in the White House giving away the Phoenix Force identity?

"This is a conference call," the President added. "I will blank out each of you when necessary to avoid compromising anyone's identity.

"If you wish to speak, touch the button on your phone. All others will be cut off temporarily." The President paused to guarantee his composure.

"First, you have all heard the news. If not, signal me. All right, everyone knows. Okay, all of you need to know that every Secret Service man with the President elect is dead or so severely wounded that he is out of action. So far Stephen Shaw has not been identified among the dead. We have other reasons to believe he was kidnapped rather than assassinated. No one has claimed to have abducted him as yet.

"I do not believe I am overstating the case when I say that this presents us with a worldwide crisis. No one can guess what we will be forced to do in order to rescue Shaw and restructure our posture as a world power. No one, individual terrorists or renegade nations, can be allowed to embarrass us internationally without a strong, decisive response on our part.

"Second, we face a constitutional crisis if Shaw is not returned before inauguration. We have laws to deal with the death or incapacity of a President-elect, but there are political opportunists who might throw the matter into the courts or otherwise cripple the administration. Whose finger would be poised above the doomsday button is anybody's guess. So he must be found and returned.

"Now to immediate response. Our embassy is to fill in the security gap until we can get personnel from my staff to the scene. These Secret Service personnel are already airborne. CIA and the NSA... I want you to quadruple your forces in Egypt. Navy, your Marines at the embassy in Cairo are to leave one man on guard, and send the rest in search of the Vice President. Army, get a regiment in as fast as the Air Force can manage."

The President paused. Someone had asked a question.

"To hell with Egyptian-American relations." He dropped all pretense of diplomacy. "The government in Cairo set up a ridiculous itinerary for Shaw's tour. They took him to some place called the City of the Dead. After dark, if you can believe it. The Egyptian president got out of the car before it entered the Dead City. That makes him suspect.

"So nobody hesitates a second. You go in without passports, without visas. Tell the petty bureaucrats that you're acting on my directive.

"Now I'll speak separately with each of you. So hang on until I get to you."

Brognola sat back, thinking he would be far down the list. Instead the President spoke first to Stony Man Farm.

"Hal?"

"Yes, Mr. President."

"What the hell happened to your Phoenix Force?"

"I haven't spoken to any of them yet, sir."

"I thought they were supposed to back up the Secret Service." The President sounded as if he was attempting to place the blame on someone else.

"No, sir." Brognola was ready to go head-to-head with the man in the White House. "Your orders were precise. My men were instructed to go after Colonel Mohammed Sadam."

"Hell," the President said, easing off. "Your guys probably put their lives on the line to save Stephen Shaw regardless of their orders."

"No doubt, sir."

"Well, get them into action. I suppose Sadam's behind this?"

"Most likely," Brognola agreed.

"It could be what's left of Abu Nidal's bloodthirsty guerrillas," the President thought aloud.

He referred to the leader of a radical Palestinian group who had been the world's most wanted murderer for years. Since his family home had been shelled by Israel, he had become a megalomaniac, the foremost assassin in the world.

"Possibly," Brognola said. "But I'm treating it as a Sadamite strike."

"Give your men anything they need. Anything at all, no holds barred."

"Sir, I'm not even certain that any of them are alive. I'm positive they got involved one way or another. You know how they are."

"Yes. Well, turn them loose on this. Unofficially, as usual. They'll find Shaw if anybody can, although they don't know Cairo."

"I have a man with them, an Australian, who has lived in Cairo for years."

"Good. I can't emphasize enough—if we lose the President-elect, it will throw the nation into chaos. Wait. I just got a note, the Dow-Jones industrial average is down more than three hundred points. Defense contractor stocks have gone up against the market. The people obviously expect to go to war if we can't get Shaw home safely. So put what's left of your team on this fast, Hal. No restrictions."

"Yes, sir."

The phone died.

Hal Brognola studied the war map.

Six spots covered Cairo, reflecting the five team members and their Australian aide.

Brognola jabbed the map with a forefinger, his lips a tight, angry line. The damned spots marked their location, all right. They just didn't tell whether they were alive or not.

Nervously, Brognola put through a scrambled call to the Cairo hotel where he had arranged for the Phoenix team to stay.

Yakov Katzenelenbogen answered. "Yeah?"

"It's okay, we're scrambled like eggs," Brognola said. "Are you all right?"

"Yes."

"And the others?"

"Gary's messed up. Nothing permanent, but I'll be leaving him here in charge of a command post."

"Hey!" Gary barked.

"Sounds good."

Katz put his hand over the phone. "It's confirmed, Gary. Sorry."

"Damn." Gary folded his arms over his chest. He hated to be left behind. On the other hand, he knew a wounded duck could get the entire flock killed by being too slow.

"You'll be taking Aussie with you?"

"Only if you insist."

"You know I don't insist." Brognola did not like issuing direct orders to mavericks like Katz, McCarter and the others. But he felt the team needed the on-site advice of a longtime resident like Aussie.

"All right, we'll baby-sit him for a while."

"Brief me, Katz."

"Okay. We've all been on the phone and in the streets trying to gather information. This is what we've got so far. Apparently, the Egyptian itinerary took Shaw into this giant cemetery, where there are hundreds of lavish mausoleums, because some of his ancestors were entombed there.

"The Egyptian government denies that they recommended that phase of the tour. They're saying he specifically included it in his request of sites he wanted to see."

"I'll check that with the President and everybody else," Brognola said.

"Anyway, we were airborne when his caravan turned through the gate. Almost immediately a small war broke out. Gunmen appeared from inside tombs that appeared to have been locked from the outside.

The bad guys cut down the bodyguards and the Egyptian forces like they were using a lawn mower. We got into action as fast as we could. I think we killed most of the assailants, but they got Shaw into his limousine and took off."

"Did any of you take up the chase?"

"Gary, David and Encizo took after him. Gary caught up with the limo and shot out a tire. It went just flat enough for the driver to lose control in the confusion. Maybe half a dozen men got out of the car. He killed three of them. But three got away. One of them was the Vice President."

"He followed them, of course."

"He couldn't. The police got between him and the kidnappers. I pulled all my people out of the area. They were at risk. The place was swarming with police. We would have stood out in that mob of Arabs."

"All right."

"All the other American guys were dead. Except for some State Department freak and an Army major."

Brognola crossed to his computer and brought up a file. "A young guy? About twenty-six?"

"Sounds close."

"You want his name?"

"Of course."

"Leonard Toby, protocol officer. Age twenty-eight. Five feet ten inches tall. Weight, 151 pounds. Graduate of Cornell. Member of prominent Newport, Rhode Island family. That's about it."

Katz remembered. "Get the CIA file. He's a member of the spook club."

Brognola reentered the name and inserted a code word.

"Right again. CIA. Works alone. He's been in that area for two years. He cut Abu Nidal's group to ribbons. Not that they won't surface again if the Sadamites don't recruit the entire Arab and Palestinian terrorist community."

"Sadam sort of took over Nidal's limelight, didn't he?"

Brognola said that was correct. "What are you thinking, Katz?"

"If the Vice President didn't want to visit the cemetery, maybe Toby encouraged him."

"You're coming down pretty hard on a little hearsay."

"Yeah, but he was shot with a needle gun. Everybody else in the convoy got killed, except for that Army major. He got the needle, too."

Brognola read another line on the computer. "There's that Army major you mentioned. Whoa." Hal advanced a screen full of data. "He was specifically instructed to wear his uniform at all times while he was abroad with the President elect. Seems he was a big hero as a kid in Nam. His medals look like a patchwork quilt. His name is Major Allen Lukes. Somewhere in his thirties. That's curious. The computer doesn't have his exact date of birth. Here's something interesting, though. The Vice President had asked for a replacement."

"Shaw wanted to send him home before his trip was over?"

"That's what the computer says. And you know computers are the last honest people alive in the world today."

"Shaw hadn't axed him from the parade through Cairo. I'd like to tail both him and Leonard Toby."

"You'll find them at the embassy after they get free of the Cairo police."

"Anything else?"

"Wait. You know your new mission. Saving the Vice President is now priority one. Blotting out Mohammed Sadam runs a close second."

"Okay. No problem on our part. I'll get back to you as fast I can, Hal."

"Wait." Brognola still had a burr under his saddle. "I don't understand why you called off Manning and the other guys when they knew the direction the kidnappers were taking. If they were carrying the VP, they couldn't have moved too fast. You said they were on foot."

"They were," Katz said.

"Then why?"

The Israeli searched his memory. "I had a hunch," he admitted.

"A hunch?"

"What if all three men separated and went in different directions? No one would link them to the slaughter."

"That's impossible. If they had the Vice President, they couldn't go in three directions. Stephen Shaw would be recognized by most everybody, even in Cairo."

"Precisely," Katz said. "If..."

"Only if they really had the VP..." Brognola said. "Interesting concept."

Katz thought again. Something needled him, but he could not put a finger on it.

"Hal, have you ever been chasing a pair of criminals down an alley when one of them suddenly stops and turns around? You dive behind a stack of filled trash cans for cover before he can get off a shot."

"Katz, what are you talking about?"

"And then the guy just stands there. All you have to do is come a couple of inches out for a shot."

"Only you don't," Brognola said. "Because maybe his partner is behind you in the alley and will blend your brains in with the garbage if you give him a target."

"Yeah." Katz was pleased. "That's it. Now you understand."

"I can't honestly say that I do understand."

Katz tried again. "Okay. Think about bank robbers. They toss the loot in the back seat of a car parked outside. Nobody sees that. Everybody concentrates on them while they split like they're running barefoot over a field of hot coals."

"And all the time, the money is still right in the bank's parking lot."

"That's it."

"All right, do it your way. Just get the Vice President home alive or you might return to a political cyclone."

"Good night, Hal."

"Good night, shit. You guys get to work. I'll do the sleeping."

10

"What we need now is a corpse," Nahib Kamal told one of his men who had survived the gun battle.

The young man suffered a slight tremor in his hands. The gunfight had terrified him.

Dawn threatened to break before they left the vegetable stand. All along the street, shopkeepers were stirring, but Kamal had worked swiftly to cover his tracks. The night before, he had priced down his merchandise to get rid of it quickly. What he did not sell, he had dumped while everyone else was asleep. His departure would not become evident until the farmer arrived with the day's goods.

The surviving Sadamites had checked in at the stall after the police departed. Two were preparing to leave Cairo with their valuable cargo. Three others were inside one of the tombs, digging.

Kamal was calm. He had stood up well when the police came to interrogate all the merchants in the row. Since all of them could easily account for their whereabouts during the shoot-out, the authorities did not suspect that one of them might be lying. Kamal had told the police that he had purchased the stall that same day, but it made no difference to them. He was definitely in his place during the crucial half hour.

In contrast to Kamal's confidence, his underling quaked with fear.

"You still have the hearse?" the younger man asked.

"Yes. It is nearby."

"Won't we be seen?"

Kamal ignored the question.

Three blocks away they settled into the old hearse that Kamal had arranged earlier.

The name on the side was that of a Christian mortuary that had recently gone out of business. No one would know the difference.

They drove into the slums of the Copts, a haven for the few Egyptians who practiced the Coptic form of Christianity. They could trace their descendents back to a time before Arabs from the east overpowered the Cairenes, as the people of Cairo called themselves. However, the masses who had been converted later to Islam by outsiders, now considered the Copts as foreigners.

Killing one of them seemed less evil to Kamal than taking life from one of his own. When he could, he killed the unenlightened.

For a weapon he chose the jack handle.

With that on the seat between him and his silent subordinate, he drove into the Christian slums. The poverty there was appalling, although many of the males wore shirts and trousers, mirroring the Western world. In the rest of the city, the poor dressed in galabias, the long robes worn throughout the Arabic world.

He found what he wanted in the doorway of a crumbling old building where the wrought-iron grate had been torn away and many of the windows broken. An old man slept there.

Kamal's glinting eyes scanned the scene. Some of the building's shutters were closed, their broken and missing parts making them ineffective against the heat. No one stirred: the street was empty. But he must work fast. The sun was rising, and within minutes the grim cobblestones and gutters running with waste water would teem with people.

By midday, the temperature would soar to a hundred degrees. There would be no fans, let alone air conditioners, to temper the climate inside or out.

"That one." Kamal shoved the weapon at the man across the seat from him.

"I can't," he answered.

With a contemptuous grunt, Kamal slid from the vehicle, the jack handle in his right hand. He did not make a sound. He walked to the man sleeping in the doorway, positioned himself, raised the tire iron and brought it down forcefully on the back of the man's skull.

The body convulsed. Kamal leaped back in surprise.

The head turned and the eyes opened. They stared at Kamal with focused hatred.

Kamal took another step forward. The eyes seemed to follow, and he returned to strike again. The body, in spite of the open eyes, did not move to defend itself.

He stepped back and forced himself to breath slowly.

"Oh," a voice said from above. "Is that poor beggar dead?"

Kamal should not have shown his face, but the voice sounded young and pleasant. He looked up to see a woman in her twenties looking down from a second-floor window.

"He has slept at our door for months," she said. "We have been forced to step over him when we got in or out. But he wouldn't accept anything from people in the house, and it seemed he slowly wanted to starve himself. You are going to take him away?"

"Yes."

He did not check the body any more closely in front of the woman. He took the man by the wrists while his timid aide came out to help. They carried him to the hearse. It was then the woman saw the blood on the step.

"Is that blood?" she called.

He tried to put her off while he wrestled the body into the back of the vehicle.

"Yes. He must have fallen."

"Or he was killed. Someone must have thought maybe he was the kind who hoarded money. You should report it to the police."

Kamal struggled to get the corpse into the wooden box in the rear of the death van. He and his helper were starting to get apprehensive, and besides, Kamal found it distasteful to handle the body, and his stomach churned.

He had killed many men without remorse, even fellow Sunni Muslims, but he had never handled a corpse before.

"I said you should call the police," the young woman said from the window.

He paused. He realized where he should get the second corpse.

"Do you have a phone?" he asked.

"No, but I can run and find a policeman if you like."

"Not necessary. His family will handle the matter."

"He had a family?" The woman was surprised.

Kamal could no longer keep his voice under control. He slid into the driver's seat and fumbled with the keys.

The woman had come downstairs and was leaning in the open passenger window to talk with Kamal's youthful helper.

"Are you sure I shouldn't find the police?"

Above them another window opened. A man called, "What is happening?"

"The beggar died," the woman explained.

"How did he die?"

Other windows opened. Several people came outside.

"I think he was killed."

"Murdered?"

"By a thief."

Kamal's hand shook as he fumbled with the key. Why was he so nervous? This was not like him.

Kamal pushed the key into the slot. He tried to turn it. It did not turn. He tried again.

"Is this man with the police?" a voice asked.

Two teenage boys came out of the building.

The key refused to budge. Sudden sweat bathed Kamal's scalp. The lock held firm. If he twisted harder, the key would break.

Ah. He saw his mistake. This was the door key, not the one he needed for the ignition.

Confidently he tried to pull it out. The key did not move.

"Are you with the police?" A big moon face appeared at the side window.

"No. I work for the company."

"What company?"

Allah help me, he thought. He could not remember the name lettered discreetly on the door.

He pointed. "That company."

The chatter continued, in the manner of people who were glad to have an event, even if it was minor and didn't concern them much.

"You should call the police," the woman repeated.

Then, miraculously, the key slid free of the lock. Willing his hand to be steady, Kamal inserted the ignition key.

"I'm going for the police," the woman said. "They might blame one of us. They are always persecuting us."

"Yes. They take our property."

"Go."

The engine shook the old hearse alive. "Yes, you do that," he said. The vehicle moved determinedly forward, parting the little crowd like a comb.

He did not breath easily until he was back in the modern section of the city, where it would be difficult to distinguish the people and the buildings from their counterparts in other major population centers of the Western world.

He smiled. The plan was working.

11

To the casual observer the hand would appear normal.

With the prosthesis unconcealed, Katz passed through the guarded gates of the cemetery.

"American embassy personnel," he told the young guard while he flashed his passport. Encizo and Aussie followed.

Inside they found only the debris of the night's battle, cartridges of a dozen calibers mixed with dried patches of blood. Chalk figures showed where the dead had fallen.

"So many," Katz mused.

Encizo nodded. "I wonder which were Sadam's and which were ours?"

Aussie asked, "Why do you want to know? Do you Old West gunslingers notch your weapons after every kill?"

Encizo ignored him.

They moved through the narrow streets slowly until they saw an old converted Chevrolet station wagon driven by a distinguished-looking Arab. In spite of the heat, he wore a tie and jacket. Riding with him was a youth, no more than twenty, whose face showed the marks of life in the streets.

"I suppose they have been bringing in corpses for centuries," Encizo commented.

The Cuban and the Australian continued on. Katz lingered. He watched the two men walk to the rear of the vehicle, lift the door and slide out a long rectangular crate.

They took it to one of the ancient tombs and set it down while the driver opened the door. He watched the pair enter the crypt with the casket.

He could not see what they were doing inside. He guessed they were burying a recently dead body above the older ones. Nothing strange about that.

A short time later the men came out again. They were carrying the wooden casket.

Why? To save money, of course. Or...

Katz responded like a tiger. He pounced on the unsuspecting pallbearers with the agility of a wild beast catching its noonday meal.

"Put it down."

The pair hesitated.

"I said, put it down."

He swung his right arm like a scythe, striking the young man's upper chest. The youth dropped the box.

"Encizo! Aussie!" Katz yelled. He called several times until they heard and returned.

The youth decided to run. He went straight into the Australian's encircling arms.

"Hello, mate." Aussie grinned. "Got a hot Sheila waiting for you, have you now?"

"What's coming down here?" Katz asked.

The Arab in the suit stood close to the box.

"If you had been running this caper, how would you get the Vice President out of here?"

"I'd use the limousine. It worked," said Encizo.

"That's what all of the security people would expect. Outside you'd have to drag him somewhere to be hidden. How about a backup plan? If things go wrong, why not just stash him in one of the tombs? The authorities couldn't get keys or combinations to locks from relatives fast enough to do much good. So why not just stash him in the mausoleum for a day or two?"

"What good would that do?"

"You bring in a corpse and casket the next morning. Bury the body, bring the casket out the next day with the VP tied and gagged inside."

Aussie liked the idea.

The eyes of the man in the suit showed the first evidence of fear. The lids rose a fraction of an inch.

"Open it," Katz ordered.

The man pretended not to understand.

Katz repeated the order in Arabic.

The man shook his head. He began to slide around the left rear corner of the hearse. Katz moved quickly, placing his hand across the man's escape route. He edged left. Encizo blocked him there.

"Open it," Katz repeated his order.

The man hesitated. His eyes searched those of the Israeli. What he saw there was enough to convince him.

Reluctantly he stepped to the box and slowly lifted the lid. When he had put it aside, the three men from Phoenix moved closer. The youth came forward, too.

He had no choice. The big hand still encircled his neck.

Aussie said it for all of them. "Empty as a field after harvest."

Katz let his shoulders slump. He had been so certain.

Aussie spoke to the two Arabs in their own tongue. Quickly they put the box in the hearse. They burned rubber in their haste to escape the crazy men.

"You okay, boss?" Encizo asked.

"Yeah. Just dumb. Come on. Let's check the escape route that Gary told us about."

THE AMERICAN EMBASSY appeared to be filled with people. Vehicles—civilian, military and limousines with government plates—lined the driveway beyond the six-foot wrought-iron fence.

More cars were parked along the tree-lined boulevard through embassy row. Many of them had the names of TV networks and other media lettered across the front doors.

David McCarter sat on a bench across the street. He did not feel conspicuous. Egyptians and foreigners shared the bench with him. They left on buses and in taxicabs. As long as the scene changed regularly, he doubted that he would be noticed by the single Marine diligently guarding the embassy gate.

McCarter rose when he saw the dress uniform of an Army officer, carrying luggage, exiting the embassy gate. The Englishman's green eyes, sharp as a hawk's, spotted the gold insignia on the American officer's shoulders. The stocky man was a well-decorated major.

McCarter prided himself on his mental aplomb as well as on the eyesight that made him an excellent pilot of any prop aircraft in the British or U.S. aerial arsenal. He was an ace driver, too. He tested prototypes for all the big names in the auto industry. On a track he tested himself. He won because he did not give a damn about living: he cared only about winning.

There was little good old British sportsmanship in him. Anything less than open competition bored him. That was why he had resigned his commission in the crack Glosters Regiment and stayed on reserve call with the understanding that he would not be recalled except for some hellishly dangerous mission that no one else would take.

Phoenix Force suited his needs.

The battle in the City of the Dead was his adrenaline, his caffeine, his sugar high, his substitute for crack and the other substances lesser men took for their kicks.

There might be a dozen majors in the embassy, but no question about it, this major was the one McCarter and his teammates had seen in the cemetery. He threw his bags in the open trunk of a staff car, opened the door to the rear and got in.

A young Arab appeared and began the painstaking maneuver of getting the car from the curb and into the flow of traffic.

One Vice President missing was probably among an embassy's top nightmares, McCarter thought.

"Well, tallyho, David," he said as he rose from the bench. "Let's see if we can put a bit of Scotch into the flat soda of the day."

Thirty feet short of the marked crosswalk, he stepped off the curb into the path of a bus. Its tires screeched. Its deadly bumper stopped two feet short. The driver leaned from the window and screamed in Arabic.

McCarter waved without looking back.

In the next lane, his course put him directly into the path of a taxi. When the horn failed, the driver reluctantly but fiercely tried to push the brake pedal through the floor.

He stopped two inches short of McCarter's knee.

"Ta-ta, old chap," he called. "Good show."

The game was divine. You saw an oncoming vehicle, judged its weight, speed, all the other variables, put in a factor for the driver's reaction time and then stepped into its path. You won if you didn't bleed.

Before he reached the far curb, he had traffic stopped in both directions.

Then he saw the pièce de résistance.

The major's car was escaping the curb.

He walked directly into its bumper, threw himself onto his back and lay there, arms spread, eyes open and staring at the afternoon sun.

"Are you all right?" the Arab driver said in perfect English. "Are you all right?" the driver repeated over and over again.

The major did not leave the cab. When a crowd began growing, the American officer leaned from the window. "Put him on the curb. The embassy will call an ambulance. Come on. I don't want to miss my plane."

McCarter rose slowly with some mock pain in his back.

"Are you all right?" the driver repeated.

McCarter rose slowly but shook off several helping hands offered from the crowd. He opened the rear door and slid in.

"Hey!" the major objected.

"Frightfully rude of you, Major. Knock a man about with your motorcar, and you don't even offer him a ride to hospital."

"You stepped right in front of us."

"Did I? Really?"

"Driver, dump this guy as close as you can to a hospital without going out of our way."

"And now, overwhelming generosity. You Yanks do have a way, don't you?"

"Look, what the hell is this all about?"

"I'll settle for a ride to the airport. No other claims for internal injuries, I swear."

"I'll be damned. Did you risk getting killed to save a taxi fare?"

"Actually, I'm a bit of Scot, old man. A pound saved, a pound earned."

And when we get to the airport, McCarter thought, I'll know where you're flying to in such a hurry....

12

Calvin James stood at the entrance of the Yugoslavian Embassy. The middle-aged soldier in a poorly pressed uniform enjoyed the chance to practice his English.

Together they watched crazy David McCarter play bullfighter with buses and taxis.

The black Phoenix Force warrior hoped McCarter would not flip out in the middle of a mission.

He could not worry too long. He had his own objective to accomplish. He had to get inside the American Embassy, where chaos no doubt reigned. From the actions of the guard, it appeared ordinary Americans were being turned away.

James saw the solution when four men in business suits piled out of a taxi at the entrance.

He darted across the street, slid into the rear seat, smiled at the driver and slid out the curbside door. He smiled at the guard and started through.

"Sir, may I see your pass?"

"I'm with those guys."

The guard appeared confused. "Their pass was for only four people, sir."

"Oh, my passport." James flipped the doctored book and started through again.

"Sir, normally that is enough."

Calvin James pretended to lose his temper. "What is this? Those four guys had me flown over here in a Concorde, and you think you're going to keep me out."

"I'm sure there were only four names, sir."

"You're sure of only one thing. They're white and I'm black."

"That has nothing to do with this."

"My ass, it doesn't. Where are you from? Some backwater town in Alabama?"

"Wisconsin."

"Well, I'll tell you, *boy*. I've got a top-secret mission here, and I'm joining my four white friends. If you don't like it, shoot me."

"Right up your big black ass," the guard said, barely loud enough to be heard.

"What did you say?" James swung around. He had to keep himself from laughing. The Marine's response to Calvin's bullyboy antics was so appropriate. "One more word, and I'm having you brought up on charges."

He stormed toward the building entrance, veered off and entered through the rear door. Inside, amid the confusion, no one noticed one more body.

James moved easily through the halls. A lanky six foot two, young enough to be exciting and old enough to be in the know, he was the friendly type. Women especially liked him with his pencil-thin mustache, high cheekbones, modish hair and yuppie wardrobe, all of which belied the adventurer that he was.

He also kept the hurt in his life hidden: parents who had died young, a brother missing in Vietnam for more than a decade, a sister who had died of a drug overdose.

He bore a long slender scar on his right hand. It was not a Phoenix Force scar. He had received it as a kid in the streets of Chicago. The battle scars were bullet wounds on his rib cage.

As a trained Navy SEAL, he was as comfortable below the water as he was up where the air was not bottled.

No one would guess he was an expert with a knife, that he had a black belt in tae kwon do.

He had studied to be a doctor, but after his sister's death, he realized there were other lives to be saved. And lives to be ended. Among the latter were those of terrorists and heartless drug pushers. Dictators and sadists. And now kidnappers and a man who called himself Sadam.

So James entered the embassy with two predetermined missions. Save the Vice President and take out Sadam, in that order.

How he or the team could pull off either segment of the mission was a mystery to him. Katz, though, had sent him to the embassy to check out Leonard Toby. Toby was one of only two to have been knocked out by a drug rather than killed outright as every other American in the battle had been.

A curiosity, perhaps nothing more, Katz admitted, but in his initial poking around he had learned that both Leonard Toby and Major Lukes had some influence on the VP's route.

"I'm looking for Leonard Toby," James told a receptionist after sidestepping a dozen anxious people lined up in front of her.

"He's busy," she said. "I'm busy. We're all busy."

The attractive blond woman had dark shadows below her eyes. She had lost a night's sleep and probably worked straight through without a break.

"It's important."

"Top secret?" She sounded as if she had heard that from everyone who entered. She looked up. Her mood changed instantly. She liked what she saw.

"More than top secret," Calvin said. "It's a message from his girlfriend."

"What if he's married?"

"That's why it's more important than top secret."

She giggled. "He's upstairs. In his office by now, I should think. The cloak-and-dagger boys interrogated him for hours. I don't know what he can do."

"Thanks. I'll stop back on my way out."

"Do that," she said.

He brushed people aside as he made his way to the stairway. On the second floor, the paneled walls and parquet floors created a mood that went with bank buildings of the previous century. He found Leonard Toby's office easily. Toby's name was on the door.

James entered to find himself in an outer office with a bright-eyed secretary in her blossoming twenties. She was fending off more than a dozen Americans, most dressed like tourists in patterned shirts and jumpsuits.

"Just stopping in to see Leonard," he said as he went straight into Toby's private office.

The room was of presidential stature. The walls were walnut, the floor carpeted in new thick pile, the desk massive, the executive-quality chair in real leather.

Usually, the desk would be bare: no in and out baskets, no telephones. Today, though, papers covered the desk as if the ceiling had been readied for painting. Nearby, on a specially designed computer desk, sat a new IBM system.

Leonard Toby stood at a window overlooking the city. He did not hear Calvin James enter.

The man took advantage of the opportunity. He glanced at the documents. All of them were computer generated. He could tell by the slightly rough edges where the continuous-forms paper had been separated.

Surprisingly, the papers listed the Vice President's itinerary for the day he disappeared. James had time to get the gist of the message. Apparently the Egyptian authorities had set up the itinerary and repeatedly refused to change it.

Interesting, James thought.

"Go ahead. Read them," Leonard Toby said without turning around. "Everybody else has."

He must have seen my reflection in the window, James told himself. "Thank you, I will."

Immediately, Toby turned. "Are you one of the new replacements?" he demanded.

Calvin James read as quickly as he could, skipping the inside address, dates, salutations and flowery words.

"Well, are you?" the protocol officer asked more sharply than he had before.

James continued reading until the young diplomatic staffer and CIA man stopped him. "You're not with the new staff." He took the papers from Calvin's hands.

"CIA," James said. "And as you guessed, I'm new. They haven't given me a cover job in the embassy yet."

"Bullshit! You're a goddamned reporter." He thrust the documents back at James.

"Go ahead. Just get the facts straight. I repeatedly requested that the President-elect's tour not include the City of the Dead."

"You've got a laser printer," James remarked. He did not have any great expertise in the computer field, but all the lines were printed as clearly as one expected of top-grade magazines. Judging by the papers from the Egyptians, they had a laser, too.

"What?"

"Just a curious similarity in print quality."

"Let me see that." He studied the materials briefly. "Maybe they have the same equipment."

"Yes, I suppose the tremendous variety in equipment that we have in the States isn't equaled here."

"You think I faked their refusal to change the VP's tour? Look at the communications they sent before we even knew the VP was coming."

"Identical?"

"Yes. And I'll have my secretary call my Egyptian counterpart and see if they do have the same printer." He pressed a button and ordered his secretary to make the call. "ASAP or faster."

Then he turned to James. "Anything else you want?" he asked. "Copies of the documents? I can have them made in a minute."

James felt his time running out. Leonard Toby would have him figured out soon. He tried to sound like a reporter. "Yes, I would like you to tell my readers precisely what is going on here. What's the flap about concerning the tour?"

"You don't know?"

"I check everything I hear. So I want to hear your story, your version."

"It's damn well simple enough. The Egyptians conferred with me concerning the sights that the Vice President should see during his brief stop here. They included the City of the Dead because some of the VP's ancestors were buried there. I tried to get that particular stop on the route changed, but the Egyptians were adamant. Stephen Shaw didn't look at the itinerary until he was airborne. Twenty minutes out of Cairo, he decided he did not want to visit the cemetery. The Egyptians refused to make a change no matter how hard I tried to persuade them. The rest is history."

James stalled for a moment. He lifted the papers. "And all this?"

"This is the big lie. The locals sent a list including the city. When I objected, they sent a message that made it seem like the idea of visiting the cemetery was mine. Plus, they have no record of my many requests for a change. So, I'm the scapegoat."

The intercom buzzed.

"Mr. Toby," his secretary said. "I checked and their communications were run on a laser printer. They've had it for a year and love it."

"Thank you." Toby relaxed. "Does that explain the similarity?"

"Yes. Certainly." James turned to leave. "Thank you for your time."

"Oh," Toby said. "May I have your card? I must report my press contacts in my journal even though I'm probably going to join the embassy in Outer Mongolia when this is over."

"Certainly. I have them in my attaché case. I left it with your secretary."

James reached the outer office quickly. The protocol officer was politely trying to catch up. James was quicker, though. He saw the IBM computer and the laser printer on a stand to the side of the secretary's desk.

"I see you have the new word processor. How do you like it?"

"Oh, just fine, so far."

"How long have you had it?"

"Two weeks. I think Mr. Toby might have seen one and just couldn't resist. I don't think either of us did much of anything while we scoured Cairo for..."

Leonard Toby had reached the door. He caught the last of the conversation. He broke into the conversation. "Where's your attaché case?" the protocol officer demanded.

Calvin James left without answering.

13

They worked four blocks of sun-dried brick huts covered with palm fronds or straw. In some of the homes, beams made of palm tree trunks supported the ceilings.

The better structures, built in rectangles or squares, enclosed small courtyards that smelled of goats and sheep. Ventilation in the dark cell-like interiors was minimal; windows were limited to slits high in the walls. Larger openings would have provided better lighting and air, but would not have protected against the dry, intense heat outside.

In the streets, a mixed odor caused by the close living assaulted the nostrils.

Doggedly Katz and Encizo knocked on every door, pretending to be police officers as they questioned the residents.

Had they been home the night before? Had they heard the shooting? Had they gone into the street to see what was happening? Had they seen three men running up the street from the direction of the cemetery?

The answers, except for the last, were consistent. Yes, they had been home. Yes, they had heard the shooting. Yes, they had gone into the street, many as far as the battleground.

Only two, a young girl and a burly man who looked as though he had seen a lot of hard work recalled seeing three men running together through the street.

Could they recognize them again? No, it was dark.

Were two of the men holding or pushing the third? No.

Katz persisted. In the end he was convinced that the Vice President had not struggled to escape.

When they were finished, they sat on a low fence that overlooked the City of the Dead. Aussie had gone somewhere to get a map.

"The Vice President doesn't struggle," Encizo mused. "Strange."

Katz played the devil's advocate. "He could have been dazed by the drugs. His captors could have held a gun on him, threatening to shoot him if he did not cooperate. There are many possible explanations."

"Yes, the man could have been a coward," Encizo responded.

The contemplation ceased as the Australian returned with a roll of paper under his arm.

"Scare up any quail, mates?" He settled between them with no follow-up on his own question. Instead he unrolled a large map. "The City of the Dead," he said proudly. "From the vaults of the city government. That will be a hundred-dollar item on my expense account."

"A fifty-dollar bribe to get the map from the city," Katz said.

"And fifty for me. A fair dinkum markup for a retailer, these days, I should say. A point of interest, too. I was the third person to pick up a copy in the past two weeks. The last request before that was made in 1962."

"Interesting," Encizo said.

"The police and Sadam's man," Katz suggested.

"A young woman two weeks ago."

"Did you learn anything about the woman?"

"She wore traditional clothes, veil included. Had hazel eyes, five foot two. But back to the map. There it is. Every street and alley."

"They're all alleys," Encizo said.

"True. But you can see here...." He pointed near the center of the map. "That's where the battle took place. Over here is the gate the limousine escaped through. And, for your edification, these notes show the name of the family occupying each tomb."

Encizo said he could not read it. "It looks like chicken scratches."

"It's in Arabic," Katz pointed out. "Can you read it?"

Aussie shook his head. "Sorry. I can speak it fairly well, but reading is another matter. Especially handwriting that might go back a few hundred years."

Katz continued studying. He pointed out the faint parallel lines running down the center of some streets.

"Ancient sewers," Aussie said.

Katz looked interested until the Australian put up a hand to damper the hope.

"There are no drains or other ways to enter the sewers from the cemetery itself. Once the sewers brought water into the city. Naturally people preferred fluoride to decaying bodies in their water. Now they have been abandoned." He raised his hand to fend off a question. "Last night a luckless platoon of rookie police officers went into the sewers, checked them out. They found nothing of consequence. Now they are taking turns being sick and guarding the known exits. All of which explains why the police obtained a copy of the map last night."

"Damn!" Katz stood up. "Still, we should check out those sewers for ourselves."

"What's this 'we' bit?" Aussie asked.

"You wanted to be one of the team."

"I do."

"We take turns bleeding."

"I can't believe my turn has come up so quickly."

Encizo had stood up, too. He had seen some activity at one of the exits. "Another hearse," he said, pointing.

"The same one that came in earlier." Katz didn't know whether he should be excited or uninterested. A funeral home might bring several bodies per day to the final resting place. Or this could be a big break for their mission. "I don't think they've seen us yet. Let's get out of sight."

Before the old vehicle stopped, the three had moved closer and climbed to the top of a building where they could not be seen.

The station wagon did not go to the same tomb as it had before.

Katz probed the scene with X-ray eyes. The same driver and his young assistant were delivering a casket, just as they had done earlier.

Today, though, a rod had been secured to each end of the coffin, perhaps for easier carrying. And a package lay on top of the box. It was round like a loaf of bread and wrapped in newspaper. Both men had coffee mugs on top.

"They're going to eat in there?" Encizo said with disgust.

Katz signaled his teammate to be quiet.

He watched the older of the two men reach for the handle of the mausoleum door. They entered the inner sanctum.

"Something's wrong," Katz said.

"What?" Encizo crawled closer.

"The casket," Katz said. "The older of the two held up his end of the coffin with one hand and reached for the door with the other."

"You think it's empty?"

"Yes."

"Then they'll bring the casket out again. With the Vice President inside." Aussie became engrossed with the closed door.

The nerves of each man drew taut.

They were on to something. They might be minutes from a fierce, ugly encounter.

"I've never thought Sadam's men took Shaw out in the Cadillac," Katz explained. "If they had, after they abandoned it, people would have seen two men carrying or pulling a third man between them."

Encizo said, "But nobody saw that."

"You think Shaw was held in one of these places?" Aussie said. Intensity replaced his laid-back manner.

"That's a possibility. There was no urgency to get Shaw out of the cemetery. If they were caught, at worst they'd put a gun to the VP's head and walk out of here, straight through the surviving security people. But that would be a last-hope, contingency plan. The point is, getting him out fast was not all important."

"It will be when the police finish looking inside every one of these buildings."

"Are you going to go down and look inside the coffin when they bring it out?" Encizo asked.

"Damn right I am." Katz grew more tense. "They didn't even use a key."

Encizo grinned. "You mean a corpse got up and answered the door?"

"No, it probably means there was somebody inside. God knows how many men are in there. Encizo, when they come out with the casket, you cover the kid. Aussie, kill the driver if he doesn't open the casket immediately. I'll take out anybody inside. And if you see anyone trying to put a bullet into the casket, that one takes all our attention.

"So off the roof. Take up positions. I'm going to stay here."

As the others left, Katz scanned what he could see of the cemetery.

He saw no one.

A worldwide crisis was coming to an end here, a tiny plot of land reserved for the dead, and just three men to prevent catastrophe.

He hoped he could pull it off.

14

Katz held a Beretta 92-F, a 9 mm semiautomatic built from the ground up as a military weapon. Years of research, test and modification had resulted in a gun a man could depend upon.

It was not the automatic he usually preferred. He had settled on one Aussie had brought to the hotel. Katz had no misgivings as he waited to put it into action.

His hand was steady as he waited.

The Beretta's hammer was back. There was a shell in the chamber and fifteen others in the clip. Additional clips strapped to his body were concealed under his shirt, which was not tucked in.

He was ready.

The moments dragged. He tried to recall how long it had taken for the undertakers—probably phoney—to plant the last body.

He glanced at his watch. Five minutes had passed. They would not be out yet. Katz could see the Cuban was getting restless, too. He probably wanted to rush the tomb. With three of them and the advantage of surprise, they could probably take out as many as four or five men outside.

Unfortunately, one of them might be the Vice President.

Wait. Take your time, he lectured himself. Maybe all those inside would come out at once, not suspecting that they were under surveillance. If Aussie was any good, he and Encizo could get three apiece before the kidnappers cleared their weapons from their holsters.

It was best to wait and be patient.

He checked his watch.

What the hell were the Sadamites doing in there? How long did it take to lift a man into a box and carry him out?

Katz thought of what he would do if he were in their position. He would have men on the outside, ready to cut down any police or government agents waiting outside.

He couldn't resist. Slowly, he turned his head. He could see no one, but maybe they were being surrounded by a pincers maneuver.

Getting it set up—that might explain the delay.

He just decided that he'd have to go in. Tell Aussie and Encizo to provide covering fire.

The sooner the better.

Then an explosion seemed to shake the earth. Dust belted from the edges of the door to the tomb.

"Damn!"

Katz bolted from his hiding place and crossed the narrow street. Aussie functioned like a longtime member of the team. He leaped into an exposed position. When the door opened his Beretta 92-F would be aimed squarely through the opening.

"Stay back," Katz yelled to Encizo. They needed one man in reserve or someone might get behind them.

Katz grabbed the elaborate door handle, made of expensive brass, and yanked. The door did not budge.

He could hear frantic voices from inside. Men shouted in Arabic. There was choking and gagging. A gritty scraping sounded like something was being moved.

So that was it. Katz saw it now.

He lifted the lock. It still held. Whatever secured the door was inside. The lock was window dressing.

"Encizo, Aussie, over here. We have to shoot our way in."

Neither hesitated.

They dashed forward to positions on the same side of the door to avoid one another's ricochets. Since the 9 mm slugs lacked armor-piercing strength, they chose to blast at the edge of the stone wall where it met the door. Every shot chipped away a big piece of stone and bits of the metal door.

But every second also brought police officers closer. Some were bound to be converging upon the site of the explosion.

He could see one of them running from the gate.

He put his gun closer to the stone. So did James. Now chips of stone tore at their knuckles.

An officer was running toward them from the gate. He stopped, lowered an M-16 and started to fire.

Encizo swung, aimed and fired.

The young cop dived for cover.

Another officer pulled up short, dived behind a building.

"That bought us thirty seconds," Katz told the others.

Katz grabbed the door handle again and pulled. This time, the door gave way on the first try. The team members went sprawling backward into the street when the door flew open.

Aussie gave up his safer position to give them cover.

They went in shooting. For a moment, a kerosene lantern illuminated the rock walls of the enclosure. The scene was not what Katz expected.

Piles of loose dirt reached to the ceiling. Here and there bones protruded. A skull stared at them from the bottom of one pile.

Katz recognized the situation.

He whirled toward a flat, dirt-free area. He saw the hole large enough for men to crawl through.

He fired down into the void.

He could hear men shouting beneath them.

"They dug a hole into the sewers."

Clever, Katz thought. The kidnappers, probably Mohammed Sadam's gang of terrorists, had obviously driven off in the limousine the previous night with one of their own acting as decoy.

In all of the confusion, they had brought the Vice President here and held him captive in the tomb while they dug an escape tunnel. They had waited out the night while police searched the obvious escape route, the old sewers.

Now they had finished their tunnel to the sewers by blasting through whatever form of pipe had once carried sewage from the city. And they were escaping.

"Let's go," Katz shouted. "Down the tunnel."

Aussie went first, usurping the dangerous position Katz had reserved for himself. Before he followed, Katz took time to confirm an observation.

One thing was missing: the wooden coffin—although a recently dead body lay like a broken mannequin against a heap of soil.

The pieces fell into place. It was a clever scheme.

The rods he had seen on both ends of the coffin were not handles for easy carrying. They were axles. The rounded package held wheels. Fitted over the axles, they mobilized the coffin in which the tormented President-elect no doubt rode.

"Which direction?" Aussie asked from the sewer.

Katz was directly behind him now.

Encizo had stayed at the opening of the tunnel. He would hold back the police as long as he could. He had the lantern in front of him, ready for his last stand.

At the junction of the tunnel Katz tried to hear voices or the movement of feet in the four-foot-wide tube.

He heard rats. He heard the rattle of wheels being pulled over the slimy bottom. Sounds came from somewhere, but he could not determine the direction.

As he recalled from the map, once outside the cemetery, the sewer course twisted like a giant colon.

"Which is the longest way?" he asked Aussie.

"The longest?"

"Yes."

"To the east."

"To our left as we entered?" Katz asked.

"Yeah. It's much farther to the east."

"Then go that way."

"Okay. If you have some reason for that, I'm in for the pot."

Katz had a reason.

Unless the Sadam gang were going to transport their captive a long distance, they would not have taken the added risk of transforming the coffin into a cart. They could have dragged a bound or unconscious man for a reasonable distance.

"Okay, let's go," he ordered.

"I got a light," the Aussie said. "Want me to use it?"

"Why not just shoot yourself and save the batteries?"

"I get your meaning."

Then they were moving into total darkness. The last light from the tomb was lost when the sewer made its first turn.

The floor was thick with mud. Rodents, rats probably, ran over their shoes. Slimy, unseen cords caressed their faces. Bits of debris dropped into their hair and softly pelted their skin.

Periodically there were tight spaces to be negotiated, places where the ceiling had fallen or where trash had built up on the floor.

The smells were sickening. Gas. The stink of decay. And always the fear that the ceiling might collapse, blocking them in for eternity.

Behind them Encizo could no longer hold off the police, who were armed with stun grenades. As a delaying tactic, he fired at the lantern, spilling the fuel. It burst into flames and turned the tomb into an inferno.

The blazing fuel held the authorities away long enough for him to enter the sewers and catch up with his partners. He reached them just as tragedy struck.

Both Aussie and Katz had given up caution. Success, alluring and seductive, seemed so close.

Crouched until their back muscles screamed for relief, they ran through the dark, falling repeatedly. The banged elbows and the bumped heads were painful, but the muck that plastered them was more bothersome. Undaunted, they scrambled forward at maximum pace, closing the distance between them and Sadam's unit.

The kidnappers were handicapped by their hostage. They could not pull him as fast as their pursuers could run.

Twice a voice shouted at them in English, "Stop, or we'll kill the Vice President." The voice echoed through the chamber.

"Go to hell," Katz shouted.

He had no fear for the captive. The terrorists' only hope of escaping alive depended on their single bargaining chip.

"I'm serious," the voice called out of the darkness. "Another step and he's dead."

"Go ahead," Katz shouted back. "I didn't vote for him."

Then in the total darkness, moving too fast to even guess how far ahead the enemy was, Aussie slammed against a wall as the tunnel took a sharp curve. Something rattled.

While Katz was still staggering into the turn, an automatic weapon started spitting flame from far ahead.

Aussie cried out. Katz could hear him stumbling against the wall only a few feet ahead.

The Israeli tried to reach him, but Aussie called to him.

"Get down behind me, Katz. Get down," the big Australian said urgently.

Katz could do nothing but flatten himself to the tunnel floor.

The machine gun was still blasting, the bullets zinging above him like jet fighters buzzing a target.

"Shoot for the muzzle-flash," Aussie yelled. The words blended into a scream of pain.

Katz fired, aiming just back of the flash. He steeled himself for the bullets that never hit home. When he realized why, his heart sank. The big man's body was shielding him, absorbing slugs like a blotter. "Oh, shit," Katz muttered.

The automatic weapon stopped firing.

Ahead, another man whimpered with pain.

"You all right?" Katz asked Aussie. It was a pointless question. A hope. A wish.

The Australian managed a choking laugh. "Right as any corpse."

"You're wounded. Where?"

"Everywhere."

"We'll get you out." Katz turned and called to Encizo. The Cuban was still some distance back and firing at someone, presumably the police. "Encizo, stop shooting. Let the police get up here. We've got a wounded man."

"What?"

The Australian's hand pulled on Katz's sleeve. "No. I'm dead."

"We'll get you—"

"Leave me. They're escaping... not going all the way.... I saw light. Get the bloody bastards for me... the mission. Go."

With the Australian's words branded in his brain, Katz forced himself to crawl over his wounded ally. It would be useless for him and the Cuban to wait for the police, he realized. They had a mission to accomplish.

And he did see light ahead. It was coming in from above. Sadam's gang must have had a special exit.

"All right," Katz said as he left the wounded man. "The police will take care of you."

"Bullocks," Aussie said. "Eh, Katz..." He gagged on blood. "Nice... you know... workin' with mates. First time, Katz."

The Israeli recognized the sound of death. It was an old, too intimate acquaintance of his. But now it was new and painful.

For now, though, he must forget the man he had known for less than a day. There would be time later for regrets.

Katz crawled from the hole in time to see a gang of figures carrying a wood coffin toward a waiting aircraft. The two-engine plane sat on the dry, level landscape where little or nothing grew.

A perfect place to land.

Sadam had thought of everything.

Encizo was covering the hole in the ground with the boards the Sadamites had used to hide their escape path. With luck the police would see no light, pass the exit and continue farther down the sewer.

Without luck, the police would catch up with them, and in the confusion Sadam would get away with his hostage.

Encizo rushed to join Katz.

Katz had stopped. There was no chance of catching the kidnappers. The enemy had the Vice President inside the aircraft. Several of Sadam's men were still boarding.

Sure, it's too far away, Katz thought, a smile playing on his lips. A waste of a bullet.

But one man was having difficulty getting inside. He looked toward the sewer. He saw Katz and his gun. He tried to hurry whoever was ahead of him.

Katz tightened his two-hand grip. He squeezed off a single shot.

The man half inside the aircraft jerked from the impact.

The plane was moving, dragging the dead man along until someone shook him loose and closed the door.

Katz grinned. "Too bad that guy missed his flight, eh, Aussie?"

15

Katz and Encizo were tired and sore from the hike across the wasteland. There was no road, no sign of life around them. The unrelenting landscape gave them no better than a hint of the direction they were walking; it told them nothing about the closest village. With no better choice they followed the birds.

Frequently they looked over their shoulders, cautious of Cairo police officers who might emerge from the sewers.

They shouted at Bedouins on the horizon. The gypsies of the Arab world, the desert transients had been on the move for five thousand years, searching for sparse spots of pasture for their sheep and goats. Their life-styles had changed little for millenia. They still bartered for food and slept in tents woven from black goats' hair.

They ignored the strangers calling from a distance, and under the cruel sun, Katz knew they could not run fast enough to catch up.

When they neared the Nile again, the Phoenix pair walked through fertile farmland irrigated by buckets of river water lifted by ancient shadoofs, crude waterwheels powered by any strong animal that could be mastered.

The farmers who lived at the water's edge knew nothing of the missing Vice President, but they knew enough to point to the north when Katz tried to explain that he needed a telephone.

In the post office, a room ten feet square with a counter and one chair, he was shown to a phone. With surprising speed, the operator connected him to Stony Man Farm.

There, Hal Brognola paced in the War Room, exploring his jacket pocket for a cigar. Finding none, his nervous fingers nonetheless continued to probe.

"Good timing, Katz," he said into the miniature microphone clipped to his lapel. He did not feel like being stationary. The pressure stirred him: the President-elect kidnapped and Phoenix Force men squarely in the center of the hurricane. "We were just about to go into a conference call without you and Encizo."

"Hal," Katz started, "this is urgent. We're just south of Cairo."

"Can you hold your problem a moment, Katz. I want the others on the line."

Brognola was breathing hard. The newspapers, TV, radio, the entire media were screaming with horror stories at the prospect that the United States would be without an acceptable helmsman in less than a month. Congressmen, senators, the incoming VP, judges, even military leaders were scrambling for a chance to fill the void. Plots for a power grab were rampant.

An Air Force general had announced that the holocaust missiles were in his sole possession. As acting President, with the proper codes, he alone could launch a first strike at the Russians before they could attack a politically troubled U. S. of A.

Such talk horrified Brognola, because it was conceivable. The United States was not as immune to revolutionary change as people assumed.

"All right," he said. "Let everybody check in." The map showed his men were all still in Cairo or its suburbs.

Katz spoke in his usual controlled voice. "Encizo is with me. We're just a few miles into the desert east of the Nile, south of Cairo."

"Are you hurt?"

"Negative. Neither of us. But we lost Aussie."

"He's dead?" Others on the line repeated Brognola's surprise.

"Explain." The base commander stifled any emotion.

"I'm confident the Vice President was held overnight in one of the tombs in the City of the Dead. When Encizo, Aussie and I made our way into the tomb, we found a tunnel had been dug through to an old sewer. The fanatics were escaping with the VP through the pipe when we took up the chase. It was totally dark. We made a turn and immediately came under fire. Aussie was critically wounded."

From somewhere, David McCarter murmured, "Shit."

Katz said quietly, "I was beginning to like the crazy bloke."

Brognola said, "Continue, Yakov."

Katz replied. "When we got out of the tunnel, the Sadamites—"

Brognola interrupted. "You're convinced Sadam's group is involved?"

"Convinced enough for myself. Anyway, they had a small plane waiting. They were all boarding—including the Vice President—that's an assumption. Before they took off, I got a shot away. I downed one of them, but the plane took off for the south and the bastard died on me."

"Can you identify the aircraft?"

"Negative. The number had been painted over. I was too far away to recognize the make. She was a twin-engine, prop job, and I'm guessing when I say that she looked as though she has plenty of range."

"Encizo?" Hal asked. "Anything to add?"

"No. Except I feel like hell. Not only did we miss a chance to burn that Sadam maniac, we didn't save Stephen Shaw, either."

"We're just starting," Brognola reminded the Cuban.

Katz spoke again. "Right now we need to know where that plane is headed."

The man at Stony Man Farm pondered for a moment. "Maybe flight controllers or radar stations can pick up the blip and give us a direction. NASA might help with one of their satellites. Somebody might have been surprised to see an aircraft taking off at a spot surrounded by miles of wasteland."

"Could you implement that right away, please?"

"Hang on."

Brognola picked up a phone and put through a call to the White House. When he came back on the line his voice was more hopeful.

"Okay, just about every control tower and satellite station in the world, including those in the Eastern Bloc, will be looking for that plane. All reports will go straight to the White House."

"Right, now we need a game plan," Katz said.

"McCarter, James, do you have anything?" Brognola stepped closer to the situation screen. "You're both at the Cairo airport?"

"Yes," the two said together.

"McCarter?"

"Let Katz explain the groundwork first."

"Two American men at the massacre survived. One was Allen Lukes, major in the U.S. Army. He was aboard the aircraft that brought Stephen Shaw to Cairo."

Gary Manning broke in. "Since I've been stuck in the hotel, I've been phoning around, checking with people on the VP's staff. I learned there was animosity between the major and Shaw because Lukes couldn't get the stop at the cemetery scratched. For whatever reason, Major Lukes could not make the change."

"That makes him suspect, surely."

"Yes. The second survivor is with the embassy, in charge of protocol."

"Leonard Toby," Brognola said.

"You know him?"

"He's CIA. With a success record the size of the agency's file on the Russian premier. He executed three fanatical leaders in Lebanon. He exploded a car bomb in Paris while the terrorists were still in the car.

He saved our President from an unpublicized assassination attempt in Spain."

"But he couldn't get a motorcade route changed?" Katz said.

"Another suspect."

"Yes. Now, let the other two explain the rest."

McCarter said, "I went to the Cairo airport where Major Lukes boarded United Arab Airlines' flight 71 to Sana, Yemen. That's as far as I have gone."

"James?"

"I followed Leonard Toby to the airport where he boarded United Arab Airlines' flight 71 to Sana, Yemen."

"Interesting!" Brognola whispered.

He flipped a switch and a new wall map appeared, this one large enough to show the entire Middle East. He oriented himself by focusing on the Suez Canal. With his fingers he followed the man-made channel from the Mediterranean to the Red Sea, a long, narrow, natural waterway that continued south to connect with all the bodies of water that stretched to Asia and the vast Pacific. By linking the Mediterranean and Red seas, the hundred-twenty-or-so year old canal meant ships from Europe and the Middle East need not sail all the way around Africa to trade with the other half of the world.

It was not the canal that interested him now.

He was looking at two small countries at the southern end of the Arabian peninsula: the Yemen Arab Republic, often referred to as North Yemen, and the People's Democratic Republic of Yemen or South Yemen.

Brognola remembered North Yemen as a country of about eight million people living in fertile highlands, with one large emerging city, its capital, Sana. Once ruled by the Queen of Sheba, the country was now governed by an unstable republican congress that served as long as the military approved.

What purpose could Major Lukes and CIA man Leonard Toby have in rushing off to such a country during a major crisis at the embassy?

"They're either following a lead in the Shaw situation or..."

"Or they're escaping," Katz said.

James extended that idea. "Or they're attempting to catch up with their cohorts, who are holding Stephen Shaw."

Brognola said, "Major Lukes and Leonard Toby must know something special about the situation. Or they work for someone who does."

But what they were doing made no sense. Unless...

He stared at the map, focusing on South Yemen. The country was underdeveloped, with about two million people living in its squalid, dusty towns and mountainous backcountry. The Russians indirectly ruled South Yemen. With a dribble of foreign aid as a primer, they wielded a lot of influence in the nation's only city, its capital, Aden.

Aden, Brognola knew, was decaying slowly. An old British sewage-treatment plant was a high point on the tour given to the few tourists who visited each year. The apartment houses built for the British colonialists were the only decent housing he had seen during a secret visit there once. There were air-conditioning units in some apartment windows, though few, if any, still operated.

"About the only way you could get to South Yemen in a hurry would be through North Yemen," he said. "Even then I think you'd have to travel cross-country. About a one-day trip in a good four-wheel drive."

"What are you talking about?" Katz asked.

"Major Lukes and Leonard Toby could suspect the kidnappers will take the Vice President to South Yemen."

"That backwater of a place?" McCarter questioned dubiously. "They build cars in the street. I'm serious. Mechanics gather up parts and pieces of cars abandoned the day the British moved out. On what's left of the sidewalk they piece together a car. That's the only chance any private citizen has of owning anything better than a donkey and cart."

Brognola ran his finger across the map. "From Aden, if they posed as nomads, they could eventually get the Vice President into Lebanon."

Katz agreed. "Lebanon's almost the only nation in the world where anyone would dare try to hide an American President-elect. Nobody's in charge in Lebanon. It's anarchy one day, peace the next. It will be a generation before any real government regains control."

"And another thing," the man at Stony Man Farm warned. "Once Sadam gets the VP concealed in Lebanon, we'll never get him out on any reasonable terms. There are too many opposing forces there. No nation has gone in and safely rescued its nationals who are being held as hostages. The French, the British, the Americans—nobody gets their people out without paying outrageously in money, weapons and national pride."

"So we should get Sadam and the Vice President before either of them settles down in Lebanon," Katz said with conviction.

"Damn right, Katz."

Brognola considered the price of failure. "If we don't get Shaw back and he's held hostage in Lebanon, there'll be a quarter of a billion Americans calling for an invasion. Then Syria will come in. Iran. Russia." He paused. The consequences were too awful to dwell on. "Get Sadam, guys. Get the VP home fast."

Katz said, "We'll be tailing Major Allen Lukes and Leonard Toby for starters. If they're doing an honest job searching for Shaw, we'll learn from them. Help if we can."

"And if they're connected with Sadam," Brognola said, "learn what you can before you kill them."

"We need a plane, Hal. A business jet."

"You'll get it." Hal Brognola was picking up momentum. "Gary, get out to the airport. McCarter, get over to the charter office. Hire something you can fly. Katz, Encizo—where do you get picked up?"

"Tutun," Katz said in reply.

McCarter said he never heard of it.

"The charter service will know," Katz said. "There's an airstrip outside the village. A foreign-aid white elephant. We'll need guns, clothes and documents to get into Yemen."

"My problem," Brognola said. "You just be ready when the plane arrives."

"We'll be in the Nile, bathing."

"Bathing in that muddy mess?"

"Believe me, it's cleaner than the sewer we traveled through. Is that all, Hal? Sadam's plane has a big head start on us."

"Wait, the red phone's ringing."

Katz talked to the others until Brognola, excited, returned to the phone.

"Now hear this," he said. "That was the President. Somebody thinks they've got Sadam's plane on radar or satellite. I don't know the details. If it maintains its present course, it'll be landing in Sana, Yemen, late tonight."

Katz became impatient. "Get off the line, Hal. Let us move. Minutes count here."

"Wait. Listen to this. You get a couple of days' exclusive on this, if you want it. If not, the White House turns it over to everybody: CIA, Interpol, British Intelligence, the Israelis, everybody who wants to help. So do you want it?"

Katz considered the offer. If vast armies of top experts would help, why not welcome the company?

"Give us the exclusive," Katz said finally. "This is our kind of mission. Send a mob if you don't mind paying for Stephen Shaw's funeral."

"The President's opinion exactly. Go for it, guys. You're probably the last defense against a widespread tragedy."

He switched off the phone and slipped into a chair.

Could they succeed? he asked himself. The mission was impossible. How could you rescue a man with a gun, maybe a dozen guns at his head?

It couldn't be done.

But the guys would handle it.

They had to.

16

They flew over the Sinai Peninsula, a mountainous, sparsely populated wedge of Egyptian territory east of Suez and south of Israel. David McCarter had the controls of the aging Cessna.

Alternately they climbed to the craft's maximum altitude to search the sky, and then flew low, dropping occasionally to five hundred feet in the futile hope that they might spot the aircraft they were chasing. They knew that with its special cargo and its painted-over identification number, it would avoid regular airports.

Once over North Yemen, heading for the capital at Sana, they entered the past. They saw only one good road, which had been built with foreign aid. North Yemen was modern enough to have sold its affections to all of the superpowers. Small, modern factories along the main highway attested to the country's modest success.

When the Phoenix men stopped to refuel, they encountered farmers wearing loose breeches and collarless shirts. Women wore long robes, black shawls and veils across their faces.

Many lived in straw huts. Wealthy farm owners lived in mud-brick houses that rose from two to six stories in height; the "world's first skyscrapers," the locals liked to call them.

The ancient homes had once served as forts. There were no windows or doors on the first or second floors. No one could enter unless the owner lowered a ladder.

The sun was rising when David McCarter landed at Sana's international airport a few miles outside the city. Every inquiry about Sadam's plane was answered with a Yemeni shake of the head.

Frustrated in their efforts to catch up with the plane, Phoenix Force rented a Land Rover and left the airport in search of Toby and Lukes.

Two miles from the terminal, the team slowed to a stop. Katz had talked about questioning others outside the airport, and McCarter had spotted a crowd that had gathered far off the main road in the terrace hills.

Driving and drinking a Coke, McCarter turned off onto a dirt lane that led to the crowd.

"Maybe one of them will know something about Sadam's aircraft," the Britisher said. "Maybe it crashed or made a forced landing."

They left the Rover and walked toward a group of people surrounding four solidly built hulks in militia uniforms. Three of them held a fifth man's body while another clasped the prisoner's hand. The wrist was centered on the top of a tree stump that had been crisscrossed with deep slashes from previous use.

A hot wood fire blazed nearby.

The skinny captive screamed in agony, bellowing from the very depths of his throat. He could be heard over the roar of jet engines. The people crowded around him and his tormentors concealed their emotions; they were totally silent.

Only the Phoenix Force five attempted to interfere.

"For Christ's sake," McCarter blurted out. "They're going to ax that guy."

"Like hell they are." Manning rushed forward.

Encizo had seen enough torture in Cuban prisons. "Not with me around," he said. "Let me in there."

They formed a wedge and pushed through the outer ring of people.

The ax rose slowly as if its wielder gloated in the terrible fear he was creating.

"Sadist," Katz shouted.

Calvin James drew a pistol and fired in the air.

The ax stopped.

People turned. They shouted at James. Their eyes called him the villain. They weren't afraid.

He fired again, closer to their heads.

Several men overpowered him and took his gun. They tossed it away. Other groups of six or seven moved in on the other team members.

The Yemenites shouted and pushed the foreigners.

Either they were not afraid of the gun, or were demonstrating the country's reputation for fierceness. Every man carried a knife. Being macho was more important than anything. Death was better than humiliation.

But then, the people felt certain none of the five would shoot to kill or wound. They were foreigners. It was not their place to meddle.

Everyone turned to the axman again.

The American force saw their chance dissolving. They were a football team, two seconds to go from the five-yard line.

With adrenaline surging through them, the team formed another wedge. They threw themselves against the crowd and managed to pierce it, but they were too late.

The sharp, curved blade of an ax was poised over the shaved head of the shirtless monster who held it. The ax arched down.

"No!" Katz yelled.

Bones cracked as the blade struck the wrist. Blood gushed, splashing victim and captors alike.

The hand was detached from the arm and flew through the air to drop on the ground. It was a gruesome spectacle.

In the moment after impact, the prisoner ceased screaming. Merciful oblivion claimed him while the military types carried him to a fire to cauterize the wound.

"Animals," Katz hissed.

The Israeli slammed his hand against the side of the axman's neck, catching him by surprise. He went down. In a single action Katz tore the ax from his grip and swung it high, then held it as though he meant business.

The groups dissolved. It became every person for himself. But the enraged spectators did try to charge.

Katz flailed with the ax wickedly. His next move was to whirl in circles until the blade appeared to blur. When he became dizzy, he advanced in one direction. Those closest to the blade could not retreat fast enough. When the front row backed away, they were stalled by those behind them.

Some people farther away regained their courage and rushed toward Katz, among them the axman who had recovered by then.

Pistol shots brought no one to a stop until the axman clutched his belly. His injury was a demonstration that the stranger with the ax was ready to use it, and the people stopped. They realized the foreigners were serious. They would kill if necessary. The people hesitated, deciding whether they had been courageous enough with the foreigners. One ran. The others accepted his decision. Collecting their wounded, the locals fled in all directions for fear of being connected with the incident. They wanted no part of things that had happened. They would be mute to any official inquiry.

Flinging the deadly implement away, Katz went over to maimed Yemenite. The other four men of Phoenix Force stood close by.

"Why did they do this to you?" Katz asked with his sparse Arabic vocabulary.

The injured man was mumbling.

"Why did they do this to you?" Katz repeated. "Are you a thief?"

"La. Afwen."

Katz translated as best he could. "He says he stole nothing... there was an airplane... last night... field closed... guards, they're from the same village... guards filled the tank and took the money. Villagers demanded a share."

Katz paused. "He was going to the police."

"Probably because he didn't get a cut," the cynical McCarter said.

"But why cut off his hand?" James asked.

Katz straightened up. "So they could say he was the thief who stole the fuel. They'd say Allah punished him. No one would believe otherwise."

Gary Manning knelt beside the man. "He's dead."

"Yeah," Katz confirmed.

"You think the plane could have been Sadam's?" Encizo asked.

"Probably." Katz walked back to the Land Rover.

James said, "Then they may be in South Yemen already."

No one answered. They remembered the flying hand and the man's chilling scream.

What if he was telling the truth? they wondered.

When they reached Sana, the capital, they left those thoughts behind.

They drove into Sana on the main boulevard and were pitched into the confluence of two ages. Squatting alongside the street entering the city, workers hammered red-hot iron into elaborate fencing. In other open-front shops, men worked intricate designs on leather. Through open doors women could be seen hunched over sewing machines old enough for museums.

And everywhere, males and females alike were chewing.

Manning mentioned the omnipresent mastication.

"It's *qat*," Katz said. "A tree leaf that gives you a hashishlike high. You call a taxi and the driver's chewing *qat* as he flies through traffic."

Farther into the city, pavement began to replace the dirt roads that billowed clouds of sand-colored dust in the air. The open-air stalls and street-side repair stands finally gave way to stores with display windows. They had reached the realm of the Sunni Muslims of the Shafai sect. Some of these rich merchants chose to delegate the operation of their elegant shops, so they could live in the countryside or in the coastal cities.

They were safer there, too. For centuries the Zaidi sect, a tribe who claimed Mohammed had chosen them to rule and collect taxes, had been the Sunnites' adversaries.

A few of the rich, though, stood in their shop doorways, dressed in white silk robes, turbans and sandals.

The poor went barefoot.

As the city assumed some of the characteristics of downtown Los Angeles or Chicago, policemen were positioned in crow's nests in the center of intersections. They were there to control traffic with whistles and arm signals.

The chaos at every corner showed no one paid any attention to them. A farmer could not stop his donkey just for a car. It was difficult enough to keep the animal moving without giving in to a bored traffic cop. Mercedes, Fiats and BMWs could not wait if the owner was to get home before his vehicle was completely covered with the dung-colored dust that permeated the air.

Peddlers pounded on car windows, and beggars crowded around in poses of aggressive supplication.

"How can anybody ever get to where he's going?" Calvin James asked incredulously.

"There's no ruling over chaos," McCarter said philosophically.

"Yeah," Encizo said. "How are we going to find Major Lukes and that CIA guy in a town like this, let alone find that plane?"

"We meet them at their hotel," Katz said.

As he spoke, he directed McCarter to turn onto a clean street lined with elegant shops, the sidewalks busy with men and women in high styles of the West. There were few beggars or peddlers in sight.

"Hey!" James whistled. "We must have driven into a time warp."

"And the Sana International Hotel," Katz said.

McCarter drove in and stopped under the canopy. The hotel, buttressed by perhaps three blocks of the modern world, rated four stars in any hotel rating guide, five stars considering its locale.

"Our hotel?" Gary said.

"And the hotel where Major Lukes and Mr. Leonard Toby are staying."

"You sure?" McCarter challenged him.

"Yes."

Manning was dubious. "It's the only decent place in town?"

"No, there are a number of good hotels within two blocks of here."

"But you know they'll be staying here?"

"Yes."

"How?"

"Sheer genius."

"Bullshit. How'd you find out?"

"Simple," Katz said. "Back at the airport I called the three best hotels in town and asked for them."

"Why didn't I think of that?" James asked himself.

They turned the car over to an attendant and followed a porter, who carried the luggage they had bought at the airport.

McCarter remained dubious. "But how does finding Lukes and Toby help us locate Colonel Mohammed Sadam?"

"And the Vice President?" Encizo asked.

"Actually," Katz said. "I haven't the slightest idea how coming here can help us. Anybody have any suggestions?"

The others stared at him with blank expressions. None of them believed him.

Katz always had the answer.

17

"'Kidnappers Demand $2 Billion.'"

David McCarter slid the paper across the carpet. "Can you believe it? Two billion dollars."

Katz picked up the thin English-language newspaper as he relinquished his position at the hotel window to McCarter. From there McCarter could see the front exit. Encizo and Manning were positioned on the ground to watch the rear or sides of the building. James sat in the lobby, concentrating most on who came down in the elevator.

Miniaturized radio transmitter/receivers linked the five. James also carried a minicamera in an attaché case that automatically recorded every face leaving or entering the elevator.

They all appeared relaxed. Katz knew better. They were poised to spring into action like runners at a track meet.

Other gear included the weapons cluttering one of the two bedrooms. Hal Brognola had shipped in what he thought they might need. Leftovers could be picked up later.

Before settling into a comfortable chair for his break, Katz switched off the television. The English channel, meant primarily for overseas military forces, was badly behind in reporting the year's most important story.

The Arab stations were filled with pictures of Vice President Stephen Shaw and the City of the Dead in Cairo. They carried interviews with high local officials discussing the impact of the kidnapping on American-Arab relationships. The figure $2,000,000,000 showed on a white card behind the announcer. The same card converted the two-billion dollars into the equivalent sum in Yemeni rial. The number of digits was staggering.

Throughout the newscasts the tone was grim. The Cuban missile crisis, when John F. Kennedy risked nuclear war with Russia, could not have caused more gloom.

Pictures from Lebanon, though, showed people celebrating in the street. And the name Colonel Mohammed Sadam ran like a thread through every scene in the show.

"What a lack of sanity," Katz said of the scenes in Lebanon. "They've torn their own country apart, had untold casualties in a revolution without goals, and now they'll probably rally behind a fanatic worse than any they've followed before."

"Relax," McCarter said from the window. "Or let's get the hell out of here and blaze our way into Beirut."

"We don't know that Sadam's there," Katz said as he folded the newspaper.

"He'll be there. Believe me. There's no place else to stash Stephen Shaw."

With its bold-face headline, the English language newspaper appeared to be up-to-date.

Katz read the article.

> An Arabian terrorist group today demanded $2 billion in cash and weapons for the safe return of Stephen Shaw, Vice President and President-elect of the United States.
>
> In a phone message received at the White House from Sana, the capital of the Yemen Arab Republic, a group called the Sadamites claimed responsibility for the kidnapping.

Katz looked up. A phone message from Sana. That indicated he was on the right track, in the right place, unless the call was planted to divert attention.

He could imagine Sadam deliberately making a call from his own hotel room, or his tent if he lived with his rapidly growing army. The man was a cocky fool. He got his kicks edging closer and closer to his potential captors.

> The organization is believed to be headed by a man who calls himself Colonel Mohammed Sadam. Sadam, blamed for many acts of terrorism in the past two years, is said to be unknown even to his close followers. With the exception of one aide, no one is known to have seen his face, which is usually hidden behind a turban and scarf.
>
> Yemeni authorities in Sana have ordered all law enforcement officials and military personnel to commence a nationwide search. Interpol and

American forces are already en route to assist in the search despite the Sadamite threats to kill the Vice President if any attempt is made to rescue him.

Katz flung the paper aside. "That's all we need—the whole damned country looking under beds. We'll be lucky if we don't get arrested the first time we pass a local cop."

Restlessly he picked up two dossiers that Hal Brognola had sent them in Sana. All five had read them.

Leonard Toby and Major Allen Lukes were both decorated heroes. Their files were full of commendations. Both were loosely linked to Sadam.

According to the reports, Toby had been closing in on the Sadamites for more than a year. Single-handedly he had crushed one of the evil clan's intended strikes.

Major Lukes was a hero of Vietnam. During President Carter's regime he took part in the failed attempt to release the American hostages in Iran, and was wounded. In Lebanon, he was one of the few survivors of the bombing of the American Marine barracks. He was an outspoken hater of fanatical Arabs who stained his heritage.

And curiously enough, in four of the past six Sadamite strikes, he had arrived on the scene within twenty-four hours. Two other times he was in the stricken city, rushing toward the disaster area and missing the killers by minutes.

"Two dedicated men trying to stop terror. Or two traitors." Katz pushed the dossiers aside.

"Or one of each," McCarter said from the window.

"What?"

"I said, maybe only one is a traitor."

At that moment Calvin James spoke from the radio. "Toby just got off the elevator."

"Katz." McCarter interrupted from the window. He made a summoning motion with his right hand. "That CIA guy, Leonard Toby, is leaving the hotel."

"Thanks. Everybody hear that?" Katz spread the word.

"I'll be on him like a hunter stalking bear," Manning said confidently.

"Me too," Encizo said.

"No, Encizo," Katz objected. "You continue covering the rear exit. Gary, get ahead of the client as soon as you can and tail by leading. I'll bring up the rear. The rest of you stay in place. Gary and I will contact you when we need you."

There were no vocal objections, although Katz knew his team disliked stakeouts.

"Wait, Katz, guess who just got out of the elevator? Our war hero. Major Lukes in civilian clothes, rushing to catch up with Leonard Toby."

"No," Manning said from outside. "The major is holding back. I think he's going to tail the CIA joker."

"That'll be interesting," McCarter said. "Let's bet on how long it takes Toby to realize he's being followed."

"Okay. I'm joining you, Gary. Everybody else hold your places."

Katz was through the door and into the elevator when McCarter spoke from the radio.

"Want to change the game plan, boss? You need more than two men to tail two of them, especially with one being a CIA man."

"No," Katz said.

"We could have our own parade," McCarter said.

"Our own conga line. But you guys are too young to know about that. Everybody hold your station."

Katz exited the elevator into the lobby and walked straight past Calvin James without even shifting his eyes toward him.

Outside, in the oppressive humidity and heat, Katz caught sight of Major Lukes.

His tailing techniques were primitive. Trailing within half a block of Leonard Toby, he stopped and examined window displays, but it apparently never occurred to him to watch from the other side of the street.

If Toby suspected anything, he gave no hint. The game picked up momentum when he hailed a cab.

Predictably, taxis immediately became scarce as the major, Katz and Gary Manning all needed rides to continue the tail. They managed to engage cabs just in time.

Three blocks farther along they all discharged their transportation when Leonard Toby jumped out of his cab. He trotted across a dusty street and passed under a decrepit arch where the English portion of a sign had been reduced to the blurry name, Bazaar.

It was a busy place: kids, some begging, some peddling gum and dirty pictures; women hawking eggs and live chickens hanging heads-down with their legs tied to a clothesline; men collaring prospective buyers to inspect their wares. Before dismissing his own cab, Katz checked in with Manning.

"Yeah, I'm still ahead of him, boss. It's going to be tough in here."

"And here comes the major," Katz said. "I'm giving odds that Toby will shake his tail within two blocks."

"No bet. I'll have a hell of a time myself. Over and out."

The problem, Katz realized, lay in the bazaar's amorphousness. The place had existed for centuries. The ownership of the land had long been forgotten. Possession had become the title. Nobody knew how many shops there were in the bazaar because it snaked for blocks and bulged like a python devouring a pig. Beyond the central station, it took the shape of an octopus.

Where sun managed to slice between the awnings, the air was blistering hot. In the shade, it was as if one was standing in a steam room fully clothed.

On one side of the aisle, plastic bottles, plates, pans and bowls hung from the canvas walls of a four-by-eight-foot stand. Veiled women in long black dresses poked about and haggled over kitchenware. Next to the stand hard rock music was blaring from four or five cassette players, each playing a different recording. Strains of Bach filtered through occasionally.

Moving ahead of Toby, Gary Manning slipped on some decaying oranges that had been tossed into the pathway from the adjacent stands. He wound up on his back with his long legs in a fruit stall.

Toby glanced toward the commotion the Canadian caused with his carelessness, but there was no evidence that Toby saw the man whose fall had knocked a pyramid of apricots off its display rack.

Nevertheless, Gary Manning changed direction, walking away from the man he tailed. He hoped to regain his position later.

Major Lukes, though, made an amateur's decision. He moved closer to Toby, elbowing slowly moving shoppers until one of the Yemenites merchants angrily drew his inlaid *jambiya*, a dagger shaped like the curve of a scimitar.

"Hell," Katz said.

Obviously the major didn't know the ways of the Yemeni men. Their entire history had been bloodied by excessive pride that led to fights over what some might consider trifles. The man could have easily killed the American officer and shoved his body in the garbage dump beside the bazaar. The entire affair would have been forgotten.

And the major was turning his back on the man he offended.

Can't let him die, Katz told himself. The major might lead them to Sadam.

Katz took up a decorative piece of red-hot, wrought-iron grating from a craftsman's bellows fire. He threw it accurately. The metal slammed into the leg of a display stand loaded with ripe peaches. The leg crumpled and the fruit rolled into the alley. Passersby carried off whatever survived.

The enraged merchant forgot about the major and charged the Israeli. He shouted expletives and held the knife low, intent upon gutting the offender. People crushed one another in wild attempts to give the knife wielder room to pass.

Katz pretended fear, encouraging the shopkeeper to charge.

He's probably owned that knife since boyhood and never had a chance to use it before, Katz told himself.

Three feet away, the merchant suddenly lowered the weapon. He was going for the balls, or hoping to disembowel his victim.

Katz quivered, making his enemy underestimate him.

A few spectators grinned and cheered as the man with the knife made the final lunge.

Like a bullfighter, using his own body as a cape, Katz slipped to the left.

The Yemeni merchant could not stop.

He went down.

Katz dropped to a kneeling position, slamming his body weight into the unprotected spinal column. The man bellowed. If something broke, Katz couldn't help it, given the circumstances.

He tore the curved knife from the feeble grip, tucked it in his belt, careful where the honed edge pointed, then picked up his attacker and threw him down in a bone-bruising slide that put the man out of reach. Then Katz looked around before he started walking away and noticed that the crowd returned to shopping.

"Katz," Gary Manning called softly. He nodded toward a ticket counter for North Yemen's flagship airlines.

Leonard Toby was buying a ticket.

When he stepped away, the major approached the counter.

Katz waited until Lukes left before following him to the counter.

"Five more of the same."

The young woman did not understand.

"The two men...your last two customers...we want to go to the same place."

"They go Aden," she said, referring to the capital of South Yemen.

"Good, five tickets on the same flight."

"Only one flight. It leave soon."

"All right." He handed across the price in rials.

"Got the tickets?" Gary asked as he approached.

"Yes. What about our friends?"

"They're catching cabs. Get on the phone to the others. Everybody get to the airport. Make it fast."

A short time later the five men met at the airport. According to the TV monitor, their flight was loading.

"The major's in the potty. Toby is at the newsstand, pretending to read magazines written in Arabic." McCarter had found their two targets quickly.

"Maybe he can read Arabic," Katz said. "That would explain why he's been posted to this part of the world for almost his entire career."

"Want to board early? There are no assigned seats. We could sit at the back where they're least likely to notice us."

Katz nodded, and they crossed the modern terminal with its long walks to every gate and ceiling monitors pleasantly declaring every incoming flight on time.

Although the woman at the gate eyed them suspiciously, she said nothing but merely looked disapproving and sent a few withering glances their way.

They boarded and took seats at the rear of the old Boeing 707, a grandparent of the jet age. They sweltered on the threadbare seats while a scattering of people boarded, mostly dour men in suits. If they were going home, they did not appear happy about it.

Finally a tour group came aboard, consisting of semidrunken Americans who became belligerent when told no alcoholic beverages would be sold or served.

As the stewardess sorted out the tourists, the doors were closed. Then aircraft began to move. When Katz tried to walk up the single aisle, the stewardess steered him back to his seat and safety belt. The lumbering old aircraft was airborne and her wheels were up before he began again to walk carefully toward the front.

He was alarmed when he returned to his seat.

"They're not aboard," he told Manning.

"Major Lukes and Leonard Toby?" McCarter said.

"Right."

"Neither one aboard? And we're on the way to South Yemen?"

"You got it."

"Hell. They might be headed anywhere. What do we do? Anybody got an idea?"

"Get off the bus," Katz said.

"What?"

The Israeli left his seat, spoke briefly to the stewardess and locked himself in the rear lavatory.

Gary Manning called the young woman over to his seat. He was trying unsuccessfully to determine when the next flight would leave South Yemen, so they could return to the north.

"Three day," she said. "You understand?"

"What about chartering a flight out of Aden?"

"Chartering? What is this word?"

Manning's nose twisted.

The stewardess sniffed.

A few other passengers sniffed in turn.

"Smoke," Manning said.

"Smoke?" the woman repeated.

Manning grabbed for a tourist phrase book he had bought in Cairo.

"Reechet hareega," he said, making frantic motions toward his nose.

"You smell?" she said. "No. I do not think."

"I smell fire," McCarter raised his voice. "Goddammit, I smell smoke."

Another man joined him.

"He's right. I smell it, too," James said.

Everybody on the aisle twisted around. Those in the window seats attempted to stand so they could see over the heads of other passengers.

By then smoke was billowing out from the toilet. The sight of it crazed many of the passengers. Oxygen masks dropped from the ceiling. But those who frantically fitted the plastic cups to their faces began gagging. No oxygen came through the tubes.

A swarthy man in a worn copilot's shirt and trousers burst out of the cockpit carrying a rusted fire extinguisher. He tried to charge down the aisle.

Passengers grabbed his arm, stalling him for reassurance. Repeatedly he was asked in English and Arabic, "Are we going to be all right?"

"Is everything all right?"

"We're going to burn to death, aren't we? Tell me!"

"Hell, yes," Gary Manning shouted. "We're on fire. Of course, we're going to crash."

The panic built rapidly. It conquered the copilot's guarded calm.

The plane began a banking return to the airport.

The copilot struggled to open the lavatory door. Gary Manning joined him to help. He banged on the panel, clawed at the crack along the edge where the frame met the door. While he struggled, he kept his hip against the folding paneling.

He continued even after the aircraft tires bit the runway. The crew did not order an emergency evacuation; the passengers took it into their own hands. They fought to crack the sturdy windows. They beat on the emergency doors, and when they did not open quickly enough, half a dozen men attacked the copilot.

The canvas escape slides retrofitted into the old aircraft unrolled and partially inflated. The first dozen passengers down each slide reached the bottom before being knocked down by those who followed.

Emergency lights from fire engines and ambulances added a nightmarish touch to the disorder.

Time enough, Manning decided.

He stood back and let the copilot rip open the lavatory door that Katz had unlatched. In fact, it appeared he had wanted to get out long before.

Manning took charge. "Make way," he yelled. "Injured man coming through. Move aside, please. A seriously hurt man here. Make an opening, please."

Encizo and McCarter finally saw the fire. It was quietly burning in the steel commode. The paper towels and a pair of men's briefs were grandly pumping out smoke with little fire.

As an afterthought, Encizo reached back and flushed the toilet.

"Make way, please. Injured man coming through."

Those who had not panicked stepped aside as Manning helped Katz to the nearest exit and lowered him into the arms of men from a waiting ambulance.

The attendants took charge, allowing Gary Manning to ride along without question. One Yemenite cupped an oxygen mask over Katz's face and was beginning to take his blood pressure when the aging warrior rose out of his seat and smashed a fist into the friendly face.

The younger man lost consciousness. The second aide crawled to a corner.

The driver turned and looked over his shoulder. Before he could guess what was happening, Manning wrapped several layers of surgical gauze around his throat and began choking him until he braked to a stop.

Soon both medical aides were in the rear, gagged and tied. The two Phoenix Force members took the front seats. The rear door opened and the other three team members crawled in.

"You all right?" James asked.

The response was garbled and probably profane. Katz was trying to express some thought about how long his teammates had kept him in the smoke-filled bathroom.

Manning ignored the criticism. Instead, he said, "Okay, chief. We got off the bus. What now?"

18

Neither CIA agent Leonard Toby nor Major Allen Lukes remained at the airport terminal after the flight to Aden finished loading.

Neither tried to get a ticket refund.

Again they began to play their mysterious little game. Toby flagged a cab, instructed the operator to drive around for thirty minutes and pretended not to notice that Major Lukes was still tailing him.

Having stalled long enough, Toby returned to the Sana international airport to discover chaos. Ambulance attendants were ministering to patients suffering various degrees of smoke inhalation or bruises.

Toby considered the chaos serendipitous. No one noticed him. The only negative aspect was the difficulty he had getting a ticket to Crete, a rocky island in the Mediterranean off the west coast of Turkey. The islanders—half Christian Greeks and half Muslim Turks—had fought against one another for generations. For a time, a line had been drawn that cut the island in half, providing a section for each group. Bloody quarrels over parcels of ground followed.

Eventually Turkish troops captured the island in a single day, bringing peace while nearly igniting a war with Greece, which had claimed the disputed country for centuries.

Major Lukes also bought a ticket to Crete.

Gary Manning, having left Katz in the ambulance, returned to the airport in time to see the Army major and CIA agent about to board a Turkish airliner. Wasting no time, he quickly bought a ticket and rushed to a telephone.

He called the hotel. When McCarter came on the line, Manning spoke rapidly.

"Tell Katz that Leonard Toby and Major Lukes are boarding flight 52, Turkish Airlines, bound for Crete. I repeat, they are headed for Crete. If they go aboard and stay aboard, I'll be with them. I'll be in touch with Hal Brognola as soon as I arrive."

"Crete?" McCarter asked. "You're sure?"

He could not conceive why the two men would fly to the Turkish island.

"Yeah. Gotta go. Talk to you later."

McCarter shook his head as he hung up the phone. He tried to figure why the men had chosen Crete. If either or both of them were what they appeared to be—an Army major and a CIA protocol officer—they would not expect to find the kidnappers on an island governed by an ally of the United States.

And if either or both of them had been involved in the kidnapping, they would not bring their hostage to such an island. Either way, it made no sense.

McCarter was still thinking about this when Katz walked in. He smelled of smoke.

"Jesus," McCarter said. "Have you been smoking one of Brognola's Cuban cigars?"

"Just gather the troops."

"I can't rally all of the chaps, commander."

"Put the call out to the others, then tell me about it."

Katz showered while McCarter summoned Encizo and James to the suite. He was drying himself when the Englishman said, "Listen to this, chief."

"Yeah? Go ahead. I can hear."

"Gary called."

A towel around his waist, Katz headed for the closet to find a change of clothes.

"And?"

"He's tailing Leonard Toby and Major Lukes."

"So?"

"They're all flying to Crete."

"Crete?"

"That's what he said."

Knuckles wrapped on the hall door and McCarter admitted James and Encizo.

They entered silently, listening to Katz.

"So Toby, Lukes and Manning will be there within a few hours? I think it's an evasive scheme, but I can't take a chance. I want you on the next plane, Calvin."

"Me?" the handsome black objected. "I'll stand out like black ink on a new white shirt."

"You'll stand out in a lot of places on this mission. So make it an advantage. Let Toby and the major see that you're tailing them. Manning will be able to work unnoticed if the attention is aimed at you."

"Okay, if you say so."

"I do. Get to the airport now. In Crete, contact the Farm so Hal can put you in touch with Manning. Got it?"

"Yes."

"Keep me informed by whatever means you can."

"Aye, aye, sir."

"Go!"

"I've got to pack," Calvin James said.

"Call the airline first. See if you have time."

Katz turned away from the newest member of the team. "Help me think," he told the other two. "These Sadamite crazies have a big bargaining chip. They could conceivably get their two billion dollars, and nobody in the States would disapprove so long as we start a grand search for the culprits, maybe bomb their territory the moment the VP is free. Right?"

"But Washington won't cave in to demand easily," Encizo said. *"¿Es verdad?"*

"Right."

McCarter said, "And God help the creeps, after they've collected their loot or hurt their captive, when they try to find a country in which to hide."

Encizo reinforced the thought. "I don't think Iran would chance it. Even Libya wouldn't want that much trouble."

"So what does that leave?"

"Communist countries?"

"No. That would give our government carte blanche in the eyes of the public for any retaliatory measure you can think of. We could take Cuba and Nicaragua, for instance."

"So where can they stash their prisoner and then hole up with their loot?"

"The North Pole or the South Pole," McCarter said.

"You're joking."

"There's no real government in either place."

"What are they going to spend their money on, billion-dollar igloos? That's loco."

"Maybe not. You just named the right political environment they need," Katz said. "A country with no government. Anarchy."

"Lebanon," McCarter said.

"Yes, we're right back to our first idea. There's peace in Lebanon at the moment, but the place would go wild with a Vice President to hold hostage."

The telephone signaled softly, and Katz answered it. "Yes."

"Brognola here. What's going on over there?"

"Plenty. Three of us are headed for Lebanon as soon as I can get you off the line."

"Lebanon? Leonard Toby informed his superiors two hours ago that he's learned the kidnappers will land on Crete by tomorrow morning at the latest. He's on his way there now. He'll be reinforced by American and Turkish forces."

"They'll be hunting in the wrong place on the wrong night. I still say they're headed for Lebanon."

"You'll have a hell of a time getting the Vice President out alive in that battleground."

"I know. That's why they'll be headed there."

"Okay. You know what you're doing. Just keep me informed."

"If James hasn't told you yet, he and Manning will be in Crete just to hedge my bets. We'll be on the next flight to Beirut from Sana."

"You'll want the usual supplies?"

"Weapons only. And the addresses of three safehouses on the remote possibility we might need to hole up."

"Three?"

"I'm not taking a chance by putting all my eggs in one basket."

"Okay, Katz. Anything else?"

"I want a fast car and driver at the airport. And three good motorcycles. And local guides. One Christian, one Shiite, one moderate. Have them meet us at the airport."

"No problem," said Brognola. "There's not much we wouldn't do to rescue the Vice President."

"Gangs have been holding hostages in Beirut for years and few rescues are successful unless the fanatics are given what they want," Katz observed.

"We won't deal with terrorists this time," said his superior. "We're willing to send the Army, Navy, Air Force and Marines to bring Sadam out dead or alive. Terrorists don't give a damn about anything. They won't bend even if their actions lead to war—regional or global. That's why Leonard Toby thought the kidnappers might hide Shaw on the Christian half of Crete."

"Maybe he's right. Or maybe he's in for a split of the ransom. I'm still going to Beirut, Lebanon."

"Like I said, it's your mission. Go to Lebanon."

"One more thing," Katz said. "Have you learned anything more about Major Allen Lukes?"

"Major Allen Lukes is absent without leave."

"He's AWOL?"

"Yes."

"He went AWOL to tail Leonard Toby."

"Or is Toby tailing him?"

"We're not clear on what those two are up to," admitted Katz.

"Why not bring Toby in and question him?" Brognola suggested.

"Sound idea. But not yet. Right now, he's helping us tail Lukes."

"Okay, keep me informed."

"Of course."

Katz hung up and turned to McCarter and Encizo.

"Pack," he ordered. "We go on the next flight to Beirut. Pack fast and light. We're headed into no-man's-land."

19

Beirut, Lebanon, was a forest of cranes. Around the cranes, bulldozers and trucks worked to clear away the rubble accumulated during the civil war that had raged for more than a decade.

Today, optimism reigned.

A month had gone by since the last car bomb. A kamikaze driver had crashed the vehicle through the gates of a foreign legation and killed himself and half the people inside. Mortars supplied by the Syrians had stopped dropping their deadly eggs on the streets.

Although eventually doomed to fail, there was an undeclared truce between the Syrians, the powerless Lebanese government and the dozen independent militias who fought the Christians, the Jews and one another.

They were waiting.

Sadam was coming.

There was no doubt Sadam, whoever he was, had captured the attention of the rank and file. He was in possession of the biggest trophy ever captured: the Vice President of the United States. That trophy was easily worth two billion dollars, and perhaps much more as a bargaining chip in the biggest game of all—war.

Regardless of what the average Lebanese wanted, power and all-out war were what the militias craved. Sadam, with his daring strikes, had caught the attention of terrorists everywhere. Now he had the largest stack of poker chips on the world table. And he was about to push his entire holdings into the pot. Every crazed idiot with a gun in Beirut would want to bet with the winner.

It was into this hypertense and volatile city that Phoenix Force was about to descend.

From the air, Katz looked down and reminisced.

"Beirut was the Paris of the Middle East once," he said. "There were cranes and construction equipment then, too, but they were building all-glass hotels with swimming pools and luxurious gardens. Over there was the Holiday Inn." He pointed to a building with gaping holes up and down its sides. "It was fairly new when the craziness started. French, English, Americans...they all holed up in the Holiday Inn when the first shelling cracked the peace.

"Before the senseless fighting, Beirut was in a way following the style of Switzerland. Banking, the world of finance, a center for the Middle East. I'm talking about billions of dollars in oil money that poured in here weekly. The upper classes lived in suites, the middle classes in new high-rise apartments. The poor lived in brick houses of only two or three rooms, but they could see the richer places and knew they had a chance of climbing the status ladder."

"Beautiful beaches, too," Rafael Encizo said. He thought of his own island home and his hopes for the future when he fought alongside Fidel Castro. He remembered the disillusionment that set in when he realized he had helped bury Cuba under a Communist dictatorship.

"Now, look at it," Katz said sadly, in spite of a few signs of new construction in the city.

"What are they always fighting about?" David McCarter said, shaking his head.

Katz answered that Lebanon was a small coastal nation on the east end of the Mediterranean Sea; with Israel on the south and the Jewish nation's archenemy Syria on the east and north, it presently sat on a powder keg. But he added that for more than four thousand years, the country had been a center of world trade.

"Christians and Muslims had lived in adjoining neighborhoods," Katz continued. "Until a minor squabble over which group would control various governmental posts grew into a shooting match. At first the Muslims and Christians shot at each other. Then the Shiite Muslims began shooting at the Sunni sect. And then the Druse—that's a secret Muslim sect—started shooting at everybody else.

"President Eisenhower sent in the Marines once when the shooting escalated," Katz continued thoughtfully. "It calmed the waters. When Reagan sent in troops to keep the peace, they got blown out of the place with hundreds of casualties."

"What makes the little buggers think it's time to rebuild now?" McCarter asked.

"Ants," Encizo said. "Step on an anthill, and before you take two more steps, they're rebuilding."

"And you think the Sadamites are going to bring their hostage here?" McCarter said.

"I can't think of a better place."

The wheels of the aircraft touched concrete and the engines reversed. They slowed along a runway scarred with patches.

They stepped from the Boeing 747, not onto an enclosed, air-conditioned ramp but down a badly bent staircase on wheels. The late-afternoon sun burned their faces. The air would not cool much even after the sun disappeared.

Carrying their own luggage they entered the terminal, which consisted of the remaining third of a badly damaged building. Jackhammers and bulldozers chattered and growled beyond a floor-to-ceiling tarp.

An immigration officer stamped their passports without raising his eyes. He was one of the cynics, Katz decided. Old-looking beyond his years, the man had probably seen too many failed truces in a city that festered like an open sore.

Beyond customs, they found the Turkish airline office: a school desk, a computer on a card table and a sign propped up on the floor. The woman standing near the desk was sweeping up debris. "Yes. May I help you?" she asked with a slight English accent.

"We need to know when the next flight from Crete arrives," Katz inquired.

"Tuesday at 11:10 in the morning."

"You mean there's nothing sooner?"

"You're expecting friends or relatives?"

"Yes. From Sana in North Yemen."

"Via Crete? That is a long way to get here. Didn't your friends know they could change planes in Tel Aviv?"

"Perhaps that's what they did. When does the flight from Israel arrive?"

"An hour ago."

"Do you have a passenger list?"

She turned and took a clipboard from a box. "Here. Would you like to see it?" She folded over several pages and handed them to him.

The names of Leonard Toby and Major Allen Lukes appeared near the bottom. Below them was the alias Gary Manning used.

Even as he read it, Katz heard McCarter talking to Gary, who had just arrived.

"Where's Calvin?" McCarter asked. "We sent him to Crete to team up with you."

"We came via Tel Aviv."

Katz returned the clipboard to the woman. The Phoenix Force fighters left the airline office and walked through the terminal.

Women in Paris originals pushed their way to check-in counters, sidestepping rugged farmers wearing old knickerslike baggy trousers.

"Bad break," Katz told McCarter. "Calvin may be out of this show. I would bet the shit hits the lawn mower in the next couple of hours."

They moved into the street that adjoined the airport on Beirut's south side.

The bustle had returned to the city. Cars pockmarked by bullet holes clogged the street. There were a few burned-out abandoned chassis rusting at the curb.

"You left Toby and the major without a tail?" Katz said, scowling.

"Not exactly. I called Hal Brognola from Tel Aviv. He had a woman waiting for me. I don't know who she is, but she's watching their hotel rooms."

"One on two?" Katz was critical.

Manning was confident. "The major is following Toby, the woman is tailing the major. Besides, I think they're going to be in the hotel for a while. You can see from here."

Manning pointed toward a ten-story hotel that overlooked the airport. Nearly half of the windows had been broken, and shells had ripped away some balconies. Workmen on scaffolding were patching the major holes.

"That's Toby's room. You can see him on the balcony."

Katz saw the figure. There was another person outside on the same level.

"That's the major," Manning explained. "He's watching Toby. And Toby is settled in. He had room service send up a dinner tray and a couple of drinks. My room is one floor up."

"What if we have this backward?" McCarter asked. "What if Leonard Toby is tailing the major?"

Manning answered. "Very possible. A top-notch CIA agent could follow from the front even over this distance. In any case, the major's career is finished after his foul-up in not preventing the VP from entering the City of the Dead. Right, Katz?"

"A curious situation," Katz said.

"So what are both of those loco muchachos waiting for?" Encizo said. "Both of them must know they're being tailed or led or whatever."

Katz nodded. "Of course. And by now they know about us. I think we're all waiting for Vice President Shaw to be brought in, sometime tonight."

"But how can anyone get past that?" Manning pointed to a half-dozen police officers posting pictures of the American VP on the street. "I hear they'll have the airport surrounded by midnight."

Katz dismissed the police reinforcements. "That won't stop the kidnappers."

Manning said, "Toby has binoculars trained on the airport. The side closest to the sea, like he's expecting a boat."

"That's where Sadam's flunkies will be bringing in Shaw."

"On the far side of the airport?"

Katz nodded.

"Well, hell, why don't we just go over there and hide out?" Encizo said.

Katz replied, "Because they'd just land somewhere else."

Before he could say more, three men in their late teens or early twenties approached them.

"Are you the men from the farm?" one of them asked.

They were the guides Hal Brognola had sent.

"There are four of you," the oldest said. "We only brought briefcases for three."

"We'll manage."

The Phoenix team took the briefcases without opening them.

Katz thought about talking with Leonard Toby. If the CIA man was legitimate, Toby could save precious hours. But Katz understood there was no trusting him.

He scanned the sand-colored landscape. Rubble filled the gutters and protruded above fields of weeds. Here and there, sandbag bunkers stood as reminders of how senseless the civil strife had been. The bunkers were built to provide cover for men who wanted to shoot in any direction, who did not know whom they would be killing.

"We need a helicopter to get around fast," he said. "Getting around this war zone of a city by car will take too long."

"Motorcycles," the oldest boy said. He pointed to three old wrecks transplanted with enough foreign parts to keep them wheezing.

"We'll need four," Katz said.

"A-okay. You use mine. Fifty dollars more."

"Okay. You ride with us. Help us get around the city. But stay out of the action. Okay?"

"Okay."

"Katz." McCarter tugged at his leader's arm.

The sound of a helicopter was growing louder. It was flying low over the city. It was difficult to see. The sun was giving up and abandoning Beirut to the night.

The helicopter deliberately drew attention to itself. It cleared the airport fence by ten or twelve feet.

"That's it," Katz said sharply.

"How do you know?" Encizo asked.

"Look."

A British airliner was aborting a takeoff to avoid the helicopter. The massive tires on the 747 were popping like balloons. The brakes were screaming.

Sirens sounded. Fire trucks and ambulances bolted from their garages. Like everything else in Lebanon, the vehicles had rusting bullet holes along their sides.

With the diversion obviously effective, the helicopter settled to the ground at the far side of the airport.

"That's it," Katz yelled. "Get the bikes."

His men didn't question him. They ran in front of taxis and courtesy buses to the motorcycles and climbed aboard them. With the exception of McCarter, each man had a youth behind him.

"The other side of the field," Katz demanded. "How do we get there?"

"There?" The young leader pointed to the terminal.

"No. I want to go directly to that helicopter."

"Terminal. Only way."

"Okay," Katz said. "Hang on."

They bumped up the curb and rode into the terminal building. They brushed the handlebars against little old ladies. They knocked open luggage filled with dirty clothes. People yelled as the four-bike caravan swept through the lobby.

Outside at the other end, they surprised a mechanic, who threw a wrench at them. The driver of a luggage cart drove his rubber-tired train directly in front of them. Two cycles went around each end.

A police vehicle on the way to the airliner slowed. The officer in uniform yelled at them in Arabic. He wanted them off the airfield.

"Let's take the police with us," Katz yelled. He gave the cop the finger.

The police car braked, started to turn, then swerved back toward the major emergency. Then David McCarter stood on the motorcycle stirrups, lowered his trousers and mooned the cop.

The enraged officer slammed on his brakes and turned abruptly toward the offenders. The left side of his vehicle rose from the pavement, then the car flipped and went into a bouncing roll, finally coming to rest on its top.

As he climbed from the wreckage, the officer poked his gun through the crushed window and fired.

"Damn," Katz said. "I would have liked those emergency lights and the sirens. Have to do without them, I guess."

He forgot about the police car when he heard the high-pitched rumble of an airplane approaching the field from the coast.

The helicopter flew past.

The motorcycles were a mile away when the small two-engine plane landed. The helicopter was hovering above the plane as its door opened and two men jumped out, dragging a third with them. By the light from inside the plane, Katz recognized Vice President Stephen Shaw.

Four men dragged and shoved him and finally lifted him into the helicopter.

There was no chance. Katz and the others put the bikes to their limits. Even so, the chopper was rising. It swept out to sea, but Katz knew that was probably a diversionary tactic. It would return in a minute.

Frustrated, Katz skidded the motorcycle to a stop. Grabbing his MP-83 fully automatic assault pistol, he emptied the long clip at the escaping aircraft. His teammates took up the one-sided fight. Three other MP-83s sprayed 9 mm parabellum bullets until the aircraft stopped in the sky.

It became one massive ball of fire.

All the Phoenix Force warriors cheered except Katz.

He shouted orders—no explanations, just orders.

"Manning and Encizo. Get as far down the field as you can. Opposite directions. When the helicopter returns, record the angle and location where you lose sight of her. Go."

"But the helicopter is gone," McCarter said.

"It'll be back. McCarter, measure the distance between Manning and Encizo."

"But the chopper headed out to sea," he protested.

Katz listened. The chopper was coming back, with no lights, flying low over the southern corner of the field. It was heading into the dark city.

"I'll find you guys outside the Holiday Inn," Katz said as he kick-started his bike. He spoke to the youth riding with him. "Hang on, kid. We're going back through the terminal. Pick up a good city map as we go through."

"Yes, sir," the boy mumbled.

McCarter was less unnerved. "I suppose you know what you're doing."

"I do," Katz said. "I'll lead you straight to the place where that chopper lands."

20

The terminal had succumbed to turmoil. Airport personnel were attending the two dozen passengers who had suffered minor injuries when the Boeing 747 had aborted its takeoff.

As the uninjured crowded the ticket counter to learn when they might expect to reboard, a newly arrived planeload of travelers moved toward the baggage area.

The Sadamite helicopter that had caused the emergency by flying in front of the giant aircraft had accomplished its purpose. It had distracted the authorities long enough for its rendezvous with the plane carrying the hostage VP.

Phoenix Force had further heightened the emergency by downing Sadam's twin-engine aircraft. Emergency vehicles with wailing sirens raced around the airport while dazed passengers wandered the terminal looking for quiet and shelter.

In the confusion the four motorcycles rolled into the terminal.

"Emergency vehicles," Katz called. "Out of the way, please."

Most people moved aside. Several women pointed at them and cried, "There they are! Stop them, somebody."

Manning almost pushed an elderly man to the floor when the octogenarian clutched his sleeve, but managed to steer around him.

The bikes bulled through the crowd and back outside. Then the four motorcycles buzzed away from the field to a remote spot where they formed a circle and beamed their headlights at a central point.

The boys Hal Brognola had sent were evidently well trained in combat. Taking up surveillance positions, they opened the briefcases they had been carrying and began assembling and loading an assortment of weapons.

"Leave my gear in the briefcase," Katz said. "I've got a point to check out after we're done here. You—" he nodded to the boy who had shared the cycle with him "—you'll go with me."

Katz spread the city map on the pavement. Printed recently for the use of various militias, it showed most of the rubble-closed streets and attempted to delineate the turfs claimed by various gangs and religious factions.

Katz drew a line along the coast side of the airport, extending it in ratio to the distance McCarter had measured. At either end he placed X marks at the points where Manning and Encizo had stopped.

Next he examined the angles that both Manning and Encizo had drawn, indicating the angle of departure of the Sadamite helicopter from their respective points of view. Katz carefully extended the parallax lines until they met. Seemingly pleased with himself, he pointed at the intersection of the two lines. "There," he said proudly.

"That's where the helicopter landed?" McCarter said.

"Within a block or two, in any direction," Katz said. He noticed that the area was not far from a slope where the biblical cedars of Lebanon grew, among the stony paths that Jesus had walked.

With his finger, he tapped the X where the parallax lines intersected. "Yeah, that's where she landed. It needed a relatively large clearing compared to the rest of this rubble heap, so the spot shouldn't be difficult to find. If the helicopter hasn't taken off before you get there, McCarter, make sure that it doesn't leave."

Katz turned to Manning. "Gary, your job is to find the place the Sadamites are holding the Vice President. It shouldn't be hard. It won't be far from the helicopter."

"You expect them to have guards?"

"Yes, but not for long. Men standing around with guns would give away their location." Katz, trying to think like the enemy, changed his statement slightly: "They might put some guards nearby, in private homes. A man in a commercial building is going to look more suspicious, especially after closing time."

"What about me?" Encizo asked.

"You tell us how we're going to break into whatever place they're holed up in," Katz said, without missing a beat. Evidently, he had it all thought out. "Remember, we want to come out of there with a living Vice President—and a dead Colonel Mohammed Sadam."

"You don't know that he'll be there," Encizo said.

"For the biggest moment of his life, he'll be there."

"Okay, I'll figure something," the Cuban said.

"McCarter, Manning, each of you take one of the boys. Use them as messengers, scouts, whatever, but don't get them hurt. Scatter them before the shooting starts."

Katz felt the tension beginning to mount. His body and brain were preparing for combat. He had no illusions. Their chances of rescuing the hostage were remote, and there would most likely be casualties.

He walked to his bike and mounted. The oldest of the youths sat behind him. Both he and Katz were weighed down with weapons. In war-ravished Beirut, they would not attract much attention, but Katz intended to travel through dark back streets just in case.

"Where are you going?" Gary Manning asked.

"To the hotel. I need a good night's sleep."

No one believed him.

"Don't joke. We need to know where everyone is."

"I'm headed for the hotel to check on Toby and Lukes. I'll catch up to you before the action starts."

He kick-started the old rebuilt Harley and weaved through the heavy traffic.

Although there was no shooting or violence, almost every car and truck was loaded with men carrying weapons. They were in wild moods, shouting, singing, beating their chests with bravado.

The Vice President of the United States was coming.

Colonel Mohammed Sadam was coming.

How they knew, Katz had no idea.

And out to sea, there were a hundred lights, maybe a thousand. American ships and landing craft, he suspected. The apocalypse neared.

A front window of the hotel where Manning had been staying had been boarded over. The uniformed doorman frowned at the bike that Katz insisted on leaving near the entrance. The boy guarded the weapons as Katz, a revolver concealed in his belt, asked about Leonard Toby and Allen Lukes at the desk. Evidently, the major had not revealed his Army connections. He was not in his room, but neither had he checked out.

Katz rode to the floor where Manning had left a woman to watch the two men. She was an attractive woman in her forties, obviously an Arab.

"I'm a friend of the man who sent you here," Katz introduced himself.

She did not care to exchange names, either. "The two men I was watching...I let them get away. I didn't have instructions. I could have followed them, I suppose."

"Relax," he said. "That's not important."

Easing past her, he stepped onto the balcony. Looking at the airport, he gauged how much he could see with the naked eye.

"The man called Leonard Toby had binoculars?" he asked.

She said, "Yes."

"And the other man, did he have binoculars, too?"

She said, "No. Is that important?"

He smiled without answering. "You can leave the hotel now."

"I won't be needed any longer?"

"I don't believe so. If things change, my friend will know where to reach you."

"Goodbye, then."

He stayed for a few minutes after she had gone. Then he broke into the rooms of Toby and Major Lukes. He found nothing that told him anything new.

As he and the boy started back, he thought he understood all he needed to know.

21

The rowdiness in the streets below was quieting by the time Katz and the boy rode up the hill to find the helicopter.

The dampening of the sound was not a good sign. The cars and trucks filled with militias were beginning to cluster. One word from the right mouth and most of the war-lovers would merge into a single mass.

"Sadam. Sadam." One segment of the vast mob was trying to initiate the chant.

In homes and apartments, terrified families were peering from their windows. They comprised the vast, silent majority of the city, of the entire Arab world, but they were helpless. The man with a gun was master of the undefended.

Katz wished he could help them. They were so many, so innocent.

And so many others lusted for violence.

Men who fought ferociously for an honorable cause, he could understand, of course. But the Lebanese factions had forgotten why they fought. The original cause had been lost in the excitement of battle. Anyone who happened to get in the way of their cross fire was killed.

Katz hoped to help prevent the worst possible horror, that of madmen joining together. Perhaps he could stop the animals who would foolishly bring down upon themselves and their city, the destructive power represented by the American warships just off the coast.

"Do it right," Katz said aloud.

But how? He had no concrete strategy for saving the hostage. He lowered his head and strained the Harley's guts for the final climb. The boy hung on Katz's midsection like a painfully tight belt.

They passed through a section of cratered apartment houses, where blankets covered glassless windows.

As they neared the point where Katz expected to find the enemy helicopter, the reason for the pilot's choice became obvious. There were several cleared spaces wide enough for any size chopper. Katz allowed himself a nod of grim satisfaction.

Generators ran hoarsely in several locations. They powered floodlights that illuminated the rim of the hill where it fell away to the sea. A patch of concrete foundation had been swept clear.

The scene was set, Katz guessed, for a megalomaniac to make his grandiose appearance before his adoring subjects. Here, Colonel Mohammed Sadam would emerge from the darkness like a god. He would stand out front alone.

Would he wear regal robes, a turban down over his eyebrows, a scarf across the bridge of his nose?

Of course, he would, Katz thought. At first, anyway.

Perhaps he would continue his mystique forever. He might speak only through his lieutenant, Nahib Kamal. He might make rare appearances. Katz thought of Julius Caesar, Hitler, Mao, Mussolini. Now there would be a Sadam, speaking to his followers, the militant minority that would rule the downtrodden people of peace.

Katz guessed that Sadam could not wait to display Stephen Shaw, the next President of the United States, to the world.

He figured Sadam would display Shaw that night. It would be too dramatic an opportunity to miss.

Sadam's thousands of new followers would roar with pride. They would want to be among those who could thumb their noses at a superpower. They would dance in the streets, fire their guns at the sky, put a dunce cap on the Vice President, poke him with their rifles, make him run barefoot, perhaps naked, through the streets.

It had to be stopped. Nuts all over the world would try to mimic the Lebanese crazies. Hundreds might die. War might sweep the region, perhaps spread.

Katz and his men had to stop the madness here tonight.

But how?

Katz took a deep breath, mentally squaring his shoulders and fine-tuning his senses.

Straining his eyes, he could see that the neighborhood behind the narrowly focused lights was not totally dark. One commercial plant, a dozen homes and one high-rise apartment building were still occupied in the twelve-block area.

Rim of Fire

The rest of the section was being cleared. There were giant cranes and heavy trucks for carrying away the rubble in the streets. Several bulldozers were operating at the end of several cleared swaths, a few with headlights on.

None was moving.

That puzzled Katz until he saw one driver. The dead man was propped upright at the controls. He could think of one explanation. The engines were on so neighbors would not question why the night-and-day project had suddenly stopped.

In an hour or two, Sadam would not care what anyone thought.

Katz, figuring they must be close to the kidnapper's lair, told the youth, "Go find the others and stand by in a concealed spot. When the shooting starts, turn on the engines of the motorcycles. Leave them idling and get the hell out of here. Got it?"

"Got it."

"I'll see to it you get double what you were promised if I'm alive to send the money."

The kid hesitated. He probably did not want to leave.

"Go," Katz said. "You'll die young enough. No use doing it tonight."

When the youth was gone, Katz moved silently until he sheltered in the remaining corner of a shell-struck home. He slowly scanned the area until he could make out the lines of the helicopter.

Staring at the chopper's plastic windscreen, he could make out the image of two people sitting in the front seats. One figure moved an arm, the other his head.

McCarter and the chopper pilot, he decided. A boy crouched outside the machine.

The presence of the boy and the two men barely visible in the chopper troubled Katz. McCarter was not careless, but he liked taking chances when there was a physical or mental challenge. Still, sitting openly in the helicopter was out of character.

Manning and Encizo were nowhere to be seen. They were well concealed as they were supposed to be.

Katz saw that the helicopter was not visible from the Sadamite prison.

The craft had landed high on the hill behind a building that had largely escaped the decades of struggle. According to the small English sign beneath the large Arabic characters, it was a packing plant that processed fruit, nuts and vegetables.

The helicopter was easily visible from above its position on the steep chalky hill, but not from inside the windowless building. Nor could it be seen from the left of the packing plant.

Behind the helicopter, the land dropped away into a steep valley that could not be traversed without mountain-climbing gear.

And behind Katz, to the west, was the "podium" where he presumed Sadam would make his triumphant appearance.

Logically, Sadam's men had taken the VP to the north. Being too close to the aircraft would give their position away too easily.

So Katz moved north.

As he moved, Katz got instant confirmation. He nearly walked into a sentry. Fortunately, the man seemed unconcerned about security. He was absent-mindedly kicking some stones and crumbling concrete down the hill. Even with the noisy engines and the din from the city below, Katz's sensitive ears picked up the rattle of the stones, and he stepped into the shadows.

A distraction helped the old warrior even more.

Three figures, breathing heavily from the climb, were struggling up the hill.

The guard stepped from behind an outcropping of concrete, leveled his Uzi and barked an order to halt, in Arabic.

Katz recognized two of the three newcomers instantly. They were the CIA man, Leonard Toby, and Army Major Allen Lukes, both in civilian clothes.

Katz was stunned. The pair had been tailing each other all the way from Cairo. Now here they were together. Had the tailing game been a ruse?

What startled Katz most was that both of them appeared to be prisoners. The man behind them carried an Uzi.

A name came to mind: Kamal, supposedly the only man alive who had ever seen Colonel Sadam's face. Nahib Kamal, that was it. He was the man with the gun. It was a guess, but what Katz could see of the man's face and build agreed with the bits and pieces of description that he had seen.

Katz nearly intervened.

They were Americans in the hands of terrorists. It would be easy. One burst for Kamal, and one for each of the guards who happened to be in the vicinity.

But he remained still. He was here to save the Vice President, not two stumblebums who had let the VP be kidnapped in the first place.

Besides... Katz wanted to laugh. Why should he rescue them, if he was correct in his thinking? They were traitors.

The guard turned his gun on the two captured Americans.

Together the four walked to a second sentry post half a block away, then entered a moderate-sized house that had somehow escaped the war. Katz moved closer, excited. He knew the house now. It was the prison where Stephen Shaw was being held captive.

But his exhilaration gave away when he saw that the windows were shuttered with heavy steel plates and the door seemed as impenetrable as the door to a bank vault. Katz backed off, crestfallen. Every one of his plans fell apart. With every glance he took at the building, the more difficult the rescue appeared.

As the Israeli pondered, the guard stationed near him left his counterpart outside the house and started back to his post.

An arm slid out of the darkness. It formed a vise around the guard's neck while a knee caught him squarely in the spine. The neck cracked ominously.

The guard at the house, seeing his partner die, made one mistake. He did not yell. He raised his weapon instead. He never got a shot off. He doubled over as a knife plunged through his navel.

Manning and Encizo pulled their victims out of sight.

Then they walked straight to Katz.

This was disconcerting for Katz, who had supposed he was adequately concealed. But his own team knew precisely where he was.

"You see that?" Manning asked in a conversational tone.

"Yes, beautiful work."

"No. I mean Toby and Lukes. Do we have to save them, too?"

"Do you have to talk so loud?"

Manning lowered his voice. "Nobody inside can hear with all the generators and big equipment running."

"There might be more guards outside." Katz cautiously led them behind the cover of a low stone wall.

"No, amigo," Encizo said. "Gary and I have been killing them like flies since we got up here. McCarter is in the helicopter already."

"The boys will have the bikes running for us after the first shot," Katz said.

"Will we be using the helicopter?" Manning asked.

"Too soon to tell."

The Cuban mocked the apparent impossibility of their mission. "All we have to do is get inside that house."

"Stun grenades," Manning said before shooting down his own idea. "No. No good. The best we could hope for is to blow off the front door or blast through an exterior wall, and the outsides are solid stone. The house has probably been standing there for a thousand years. By the time we get the hole in the wall and the grenade inside, Shaw will be dead."

"Besides," Encizo said, "the way I figure it, the house has five or six rooms. One across the front...that's good. Two more back of that...that's bad. And two more at the rear."

"That's where they'll have Shaw," Katz said. "Back room. Back corner. Two guards."

"Toughest place in the house. It looks like there was a barn attached once. The exterior walls of that part are doubly thick."

"A tunnel?" Katz suggested.

"And ruin my fingernails?" Manning grunted. "You'd be digging through stone."

"We wait then."

"Wait?"

"Until Colonel Mohammed Sadam comes out."

"Then we take him prisoner. Threaten to shoot him if he fails to free the Vice President. And if he says he doesn't care..." Encizo's idea trailed off. "Hell, that's no threat. That's Russian roulette with five shells in the cylinder."

"Katz?" Manning wanted a plan from the leader.

"We'll wait until we get a larger audience."

"What?"

He took them to the platform, standing just beyond the lights. They looked down on thousands of armed men beginning to make their way up the hill on foot.

"Oh, my God," Manning said.

"Dios mio," Encizo whispered.

Katz said lightly, "They're all coming up here to see their new leader, Mohammed Sadam."

"Thousands of them," Manning groaned.

"But think of it this way," Katz said. "They'll be in a good mood when they first get here."

Twisted steel and broken concrete provided cover for the Phoenix Force four as they huddled near the helicopter.

Each of them felt an emptiness, perhaps a slight loss of confidence that extended beyond the enemy and the seemingly impossible mission that was about to climax.

The Englishman, David McCarter, put it into words.

"I wish Calvin James were here. If we ever faced a situation where we needed everybody, this mind boggler is it."

No one responded. They thought of the young black American who had been such a vital link in many recent missions. All of them had learned to depend upon him. Regrettably there was no bringing him into the action. He would still be on the island of Crete, trying to figure a way to get to Lebanon in time.

He could not. There was no chance.

"We have the boys," Katz said thoughtfully.

And, in fact, they were making good use of the youths. One sat with a weapon pointed at the sullen face of the helicopter pilot. It was an old M-3 grease gun that he had picked up somewhere on his own. But the pilot, who seemed resigned to his place, would take no chances. He still had hope of getting out of his current predicament alive.

"The pilot understands the boy will kill him if he tries to escape," McCarter said.

"And he's going to start the engine when the first shot is fired?" Katz asked.

"Yes."

"That means the kid will have to hang around after the fighting starts," Gary Manning said disapprovingly.

"I'm afraid so, old chap. But at his age, our fearless leader was in the thick of things."

Katz changed the subject. "Everybody has checked out his weapon and ammunition?"

They carried Uzis, 8.8 pounds of sheet-metal stampings with machined blocks of steel welded in place where needed. They were more than seventeen inches long, with ten of those inches in the barrel.

The men carried spare clips in plastic holders attached to their belts, plus an assortment of personally favored weapons, from garrotes to stilettos. Each man carried a single stun grenade, and everyone except Katz a fragmentation apple. Katz wore his cleverly designed hook in place of his right arm. Tonight, he decided, he would use the artificial hand primarily for the ultracompact machine gun. The complex hooked device held the Uzi now as he rocked back on his haunches and drew a deep breath before he began the briefing.

"Ignore the noise," he advised.

It was a difficult suggestion to follow.

Each man took a deep breath as if he intended to swim under water as far as he could go.

The soldiers assembled at the foot of the hill formed rows a hundred yards wide, in militia style. They walked elbow to elbow, guns held high. One row followed another. Katz had no idea how many killers there were in the awesome human wave moving toward the Sadamite headquarters and the miniscule Phoenix Force resistance.

The mindless shrieks of the mob and the irregular crack of shots fired in the air had died away while the Lebanese and Palestinians took up their formation. With the first step in the advance, though, the disconcerting noise began again, first the random gunfire, then chanting. "Sadam. Sadam. Sadam."

The word pulsated as it grew from the first barely audible whisper. "Sadam. Sadam."

Katz thought of the Korean War. He remembered veterans who had talked about the awesome bugle call to arms the Chinese Communists had sounded to accompany the human waves that charged the entrenched Americans. "You hit one of them with every shot," a friend told him. "You couldn't miss. Yet they kept coming, stumbling over their own dead. Those damned bugles. And those howling Chinese, practically throwing themselves onto our guns." The friend had turned a sickly green at the memories. "It was the killing that was the worst. All the killing and they never overran us. Not once."

Katz figured on a similar scene that night, until the four submachine guns went dry. And they would. Still, if every shell and grenade scored, they could not kill enough. The hordes would keep on coming in like the surf.

The Phoenix soldiers could not shoot their way in and out of this one.

Katz said, "We have ten, fifteen minutes at the most before the first file reaches the podium, that piece of concrete where the floodlights converge."

He visualized the noisy mob pressing in on the makeshift reception area. They would be no more than forty yards from the house in which the Vice President was held.

"They'll send out a few guards before Sadam comes out himself." Gary Manning thought of deer in his beloved north woods. Often the mother would come out to the edge of the water and look about cautiously before letting her young leave the protective bush.

"They'll look for the guards they had stationed outside," McCarter said.

Encizo said, "They won't find any. We killed them all, including the one guarding the generator."

"Let's hope they don't worry about the missing guards. Whoever comes out is going to be on a high. They won't worry much about anything." Katz was trying to reassure himself. "They have the Vice President, Leonard Toby and Major Lukes as hostages."

"And a million bloody drones on the hill," McCarter said. He just loved to exaggerate.

"Who's going to stop them?" the Cuban asked naively.

"Us." Katz laughed.

"Oh, yeah. Us." He pondered briefly. "How are we going to do all this, anyway?"

"We're going to do it right the first time," Manning said. "Or not at all. More important, boss, when do I disable the generator?"

The field commander's mind normally ran to precision: precise orders, precisely followed. This time he could not think of a precise answer. "Gary, we need the lights on until Sadam is on stage. We need them on until I get inside the house, and off when I bring out the hostage. I guess you have to be the judge. Now..."

"Wait a minute," Manning said. "What's all this about *you* going in after the hostage? Aren't you going to want some help?"

"No, I'll try on my own. If I don't rescue Shaw, each of you take a turn." He changed the subject. "So, Gary, one of your assignments is the generator. Have one of the boys do it, if you like. It's in a protected area. McCarter, be sure the helicopter doesn't get away."

"You telling me I'm supposed to sit on my arse and watch a whirlybird while the rest of you make the rescue?"

"No, David, I'm telling you to have the boy keep the craft on the ground and be ready to go. It's the kind of assignment I got when I started out. As for me, I'm responsible for the motorcycles."

"If we get out of here in the helicopter, what do we need the bikes for? For backup?"

"Something like that. I'm still planning the details."

A shout thundered from the thousands of men climbing the hill. Every Phoenix Force man stood up.

The mob was halfway up the hill. They were holding their guns above their heads. The chanting continued. "Sa-dam, Sa-dam, Sa-dam."

It pounded at the team members' eardrums.

"Sa-dam. Sa-dam. Sa-dam."

To a man, the Phoenix team wanted to back away. To run into the mountains. The odds were too enormous.

"Maybe we could just mingle with the mob," Manning said.

"Yeah, Encizo, nobody would ever guess you aren't an Arab."

"All right," the Englishman interrupted. "We've got about eight minutes. Let's hear the plan."

"Look," Manning interrupted.

He pointed at the entrance to Sadam's headquarters. A man came out, called a couple of names and searched briefly before turning back.

"They sent him out to see if the guards were in place," McCarter said.

He stopped. The man had heard the crowd. He stepped into the light. He moved closer to the rim. He saw the horde approaching.

"Sa-dam. Sa-dam. We want Sadam." It was eerie, unreal, coming as it did from over the edge of a hill.

Backing away, awestruck, the Sadamite turned and ran into the house. A moment later, another appeared. Then Nahib Kamal, Sadam's lieutenant, came out for a look. He held up his arms as a greeting to the advancing men.

They cheered and quickened their pace.

"Five minutes at the most," said Katz.

"Sa-dam, Sa-dam." It was closer, louder.

"Well, dammit, let's get on with it," McCarter said.

"Yes, tell us the plan," Manning added.

"Yeah, chief, how are we going to get out of this one?" Encizo questioned.

"We're bringing in General Patton's armored division," the field commander said, with a smile no one saw in the dark.

23

Nahib Kamal walked slowly from the house, leaving two men with AK-47s to guard the steel-plated door. He walked straight to the cleared platform area where the lights focused.

The crowd saw him and roared. Many fired their guns. Their forward surge halted when Sadam's only lieutenant raised his hands.

"Sadam," they cried for their new idol. "Sadam."

Then another cry rose in Arabic. "Shaw. We want Shaw. We want to see Shaw."

"Sadam."

"Shaw."

The battle of words played out in a friendly tone, but Kamal realized the crowd could not be kept waiting. Most of those before him were young. They wanted instant gratification. They were accustomed to taking whatever they wanted to, be it food, merchandise or lives.

In response, Kamal turned slightly and swung his right hand out and toward the house. Here he is, he was saying, the man you want to see, Colonel Mohammed Sadam. The man who has brought the United States of America to its knees.

The militia pushed forward again. The chant was being repeated nonstop. "Sadam, Shaw, Sadam."

The mind-rattling din caught fire, soared and swelled upward. As if hypnotized, Kamal found himself overwhelmed by it, euphorically adrift like a leaf in the vortex of a cyclone.

FAR TO THE NORTH of the house, a bulldozer began to move slowly down the hill. No one sat at the controls. Manning had locked it in gear and wedged in stones to keep fuel feeding the engine.

He jumped into the seat of a larger bulldozer and raised the blade until it obstructed his vision. Only when he hunched down could he peer through the narrow slit left between blade and engine. He aimed directly at the house, at the side farthest from the room where they believed the hostage to be kept.

Manning held his automatic weapon ready to wipe out any obstructions.

He saw the door of the house open. The guards stood aside. Into the doorway stepped a shadow dressed in an Arabic-style neck-to-foot shirt of white, a turban and what looked like a scarf tied across his his face.

"Sadam," Manning said aloud.

When the figure had taken two steps, the Canadian could see the glistening silver belt and the long, curved scimitar hanging at his side.

Here at last was Sadam.

COLONEL MOHAMMED SADAM felt the rhythm and the energy of the throng. He could smell the perspiration. He could see the flash of their weapons reflected in their excited eyes.

He had no intention of walking among them. Unwashed fools, fighting and dying over trivia. Anyone he touched with affection would first learn to be as disciplined as a palace guard.

They would take all of Lebanon tonight. Tomorrow they would relieve the Syrians and send them home.

His lieutenant, Kamal, would rub the nose of the American President-to-be in the camel shit. He would arouse the Arab world until the fools thought they could hold their hostage's arm across a tree stump and have pictures broadcast to the world showing the Muslim's ax of justice. Perhaps they would send a finger and an ear to the White House.

And just before the Americans pounded Lebanon to complete rubble, he, Sadam, might send a secret emissary to Washington. He would get his two billion dollars secretly.

He would promise to rescue the hostage in time for the inauguration.

Of course, the President-elect would have been taken somewhere else by then. A small oil-rich member of OPEC would be holding the Vice President secretly.

America would free Sadam's legions to swarm into the oil sheikhdom to gallantly free the American Vice President from the monstrous royal family.

Kamal would be the heinous international terrorist. He might send Kamal's head to Washington to show his lieutenant's repentance.

The common people of the United States would see the mysterious Sadam as a hero. They would never know that the two-billion-dollar ransom had been paid.

These were Sadam's boundless, unlimited thoughts as he moved closer to the lights.

The possibilities were beyond imagination for a man ruling selfless maniacs who lived just to die for a cause, any cause.

DAVID MCCARTER SAT confidently at the wheel of the powerful tractor that could haul away thousands of pounds of dirt and rock without strain.

There was nothing menacing about its size. Those who saw it would be distracted only momentarily.

The tractor ground toward its target.

THE MONSTROUS CRANE MOVED slowly over level ground. Its immense steel arm stretched nearly four stories into the blue-black sky. From it dangled a wrecker's ball.

Inside the cabin, Rafael Encizo sat tensely at the controls, the sweat on his upper lip belying his concern that the top-heavy behemoth might topple.

His primary concern was not for himself. He would escape. Or if he did die, it would be by his own error.

Far above him, at the very top of the arm, his friend and field commander, Yakov Katzenelenbogen, was riding the wrecker's ball like a man on a runaway horse. The monster seemed to shake violently, as though trying to buck Katz clear. But he held on tight.

He wore a workman's glove, which they had found in the cabin, to protect his hand.

Below, he saw Sadam about to step into the lights. He waved to Encizo. Move faster, the gesture ordered.

Finally, he was in position.

The giant metal ball, weighing thousands of pounds, swung slowly on the cable. How many homes had it demolished? Katz wondered. It was a destroyer, not a builder. And if he guessed wrong tonight, if it did not fall where it was meant to, it might destroy the Phoenix warrior himself.

SILENCE. SO POWERFUL was the mounting suspense that a thousand voices stopped. People from the nearby houses and apartment buildings fled.

The only sounds that persisted were from the engines and generators that had been working nightly for weeks.

There was silence in the focus of the lights.

There was not a sound from the legions of armed men who waited.

Then the single, regal figure stepped alone into the light. There was no outcry, no cheer.

The sharply inhaled breath of half the men in the crowd broke the silence. The chant began again.

"Sa-dam. Sa-dam. Sa-dam."

The voices were one.

He stood there, his face and body completely hidden except for the slit where his sky-blue eyes looked out over the heads of the masses. Colonel Mohammed Sadam, omnipotent, like Zeus on Mount Olympus.

He drew his great scimitar and held it across his chest. Its blade rested carefully in his left hand.

He had dreamed of this night for all the lifetime he could recall.

And now it was here.

GARY MANNING FED full power to the bulldozer. The tree-height blade would slam into the house in less than five seconds.

David McCarter jumped from the huge truck as it raced toward the front of the building. The Englishman rolled, got to his feet and bolted for the helicopter.

Katz waved wildly from the end of the crane arm. Encizo read the signal and released the lever. The great destructive sphere fell like a meteor. As it plunged into the roof of the house, Katz wrapped his gloved hand around the heavy cable and let himself slide.

The ball broke through inches ahead of him. With his hook, reaching up, he caught a section of splintering wood to slow his headlong descent. He entered a room of flying timbers and boiling, blinding dust. Disembodied howls of terror sliced through the choking cloud.

A uniformed soldier stumbled forward, extending his arms menacingly. Katz stomped on the back of the man's neck. It broke like a match.

From a front room came the rumble of falling rock, and a guard staggered back, fleeing from the bulldozer that Gary Manning had guided into the wall.

The guard held up his palms as if to show he was not armed, but Katz could trust nothing of that kind. He swung the Uzi and tore through the man's shirt and guts as if he were preparing a biology project.

An agonized cry told a story from the front room. Trying to escape the disintegrating wall, an Arab made it halfway through the door as David McCarter's truck smashed into the front of the house.

A jagged two-by-four impaled the Arab's pelvis. It would be endless minutes before merciful death came. The man's shrieks penetrated and then became part of the fabric of chaos.

Katz put his feet on the steel ball and his bare hand on the cable. He still had not seen America's next President. The man had to be here—but was he still alive?

"Shaw! Stephen Shaw!" Katz called.

"Yes." A bent figure staggered from the far corner of the room. "I'm Vice President Stephen Shaw," he said.

Katz had no time for niceties. "Get on the ball. Hurry."

"On the ball? Are you joking?"

"The wrecking ball. Grab the cable."

"Oh."

Shaw climbed on, clutching the cable with both hands. "Are you sure this is strong enough to carry two of us?" he questioned.

"The elevator inspector comes next week. So hang on."

"Help," a voice called in English from one of the other rooms.

"That'll be Leonard Toby or Major Lukes," the VP said. "They were captured just a few hours ago."

Somebody was picking his way through the haze when the lights went out.

"I can't see him." Katz raised his weapon as high as he could, and released a long burst. The muzzle extended one inch from the hole in the ceiling, enough for Rafael Encizo, watching from the operator's cab, to see the muzzle-flash.

The cable took up slack and began to raise its passengers.

"The other prisoners can get out on their own, I guess," Shaw said.

"That hole is hardly big enough for two of us, and I can't ask Encizo to run an elevator service."

"But—"

"Watch your back," Katz ordered.

Shards of wood tore at the Israeli and the Vice President as they flattened their bodies to the cable.

Once Encizo had maneuvered them clear of the wreckage, Katz pointed around the packing plant. "Jump, and run in that direction," he ordered Shaw. "Hide by the helicopter until I can get everybody else out of here."

"Well, couldn't you and I go ahead?" the Vice President said.

"Sorry, Mr. VP. My buddies go, too."

"Fair enough," Shaw said. "Give me a gun and I'll help."

"Get the one from the kid at the chopper. Send him home. It's past his bedtime."

Katz jumped free just before Encizo swung the crane away. As he started back toward the house, he saw a tall form climbing from the hole in the roof. The man had an AK-47.

Sadam's man or one of his captives?

Katz raised his gun and fired, aiming to incapacitate the man just in case.

The chaos at the front of the house was only beginning, but it was causing enormous confusion in the enemy ranks.

Katz ran across the unlighted expanse toward the podium. The troops on the slope were coming out of their crouched positions slowly.

With the truck rolling back from the house and turning over with a roar, men were scattering, some too late to avoid the small bulldozers Manning had set on autopilot.

Finally, only Katz and a second solitary figure stood upright on the podium in the midst of the furor.

Sadam still wore his robe, his turban and the scarf across his lower face. If he had the scimitar, it was concealed behind his back, Katz decided.

The masses let the two men play out their roles.

"Colonel Mohammed Sadam." A slight smile played on the Israeli's lips. The barrel of his weapon pointed directly at the other man's midsection. "May I introduce myself?"

Sadam said it for him. "Yakov Katzenelenbogen, senior member and field commander...is that correct? Field commander of Phoenix Force, a covert operation that people like me are not supposed to know exists."

Katz smarted as though he had been insulted. Instead he said, "And you, Colonel Sadam, also known as Leonard Toby, Central Intelligence Agency, Middle East command."

"You guessed."

"It had to be you. No one else could have arranged for the Vice President to visit the City of the Dead."

"Why me, then? Why not Major Lukes?"

"Nothing concrete. Just the binoculars on your balcony. You knew that you would have to watch for your people to land. The major was only interested in trailing you. He must have suspected you before I did."

"Do we deal?" Sadam asked. "Or do I simply let my army tear you and your people apart bone by bone?"

"You'd be dead," Katz said.

"And this rabble would have the Vice President. Not a pretty thought, is it?"

Around them soldier irregulars were rising again. They had the dazed look of men in battle when an artillery shell has fallen in their midst. Those untouched rise slowly, as if to reassure themselves that their bodies are still intact.

Before they could become a threat, an unmanned road grader growled over the ridge of the hill on an angle, scraping a growing collection of bodies in front of its blade.

Limbs and torsos lodged themselves in the wheels and frames.

Another truck was heading into the masses. The crane lurched forward at the same time.

Some of the marksmen started blazing away at the machines. Encizo, who was still crouched in the crane's cab, watched two lines of bullet holes march across the heavy glass shield.

The beleaguered Cuban leaped out, fired a string of machine-gun bullets into the field of human beings, then disappeared in a crouching run, his hand clutching a bleeding ear.

Sadam, with an automatic weapon pointed at his chest, raised the great scimitar over his head. It started its arch toward Katz's head.

In one of those fleeting passages of the mind at times of tremendous stress, Katz gauged the man's action in a play of question and answer that seemed to happen simultaneously in an expanded second of time. Madness? No. Suicide? No. The Israeli's mind contended with the possibilities. A sword against a gun. Genius? Yes.

Katz raised the Uzi barrel from the biggest target, the man's chest, and blew away the face behind the turban and scarf.

The scimitar, its course deflected when Sadam's head snapped back, hissed through air an inch from Katz's body.

"Crazy." Manning came running through the dark. Behind him was the confusion of heavy machinery rolling over bodies and guns firing an illusionary targets.

"No," Katz said.

"No?"

"Bulletproof vest. He almost tricked me. Check if you like."

"Katzenelenbogen," a familiar voice shouted behind him.

Katz spun around, his eyes piercing the darkness to recognize the AK-47 pointed just above his shoulder. He tried to drop before the barrel lowered. There was no time. The Russian assault weapon clattered.

Katz anticipated his executioner. It was Major Allen Lukes.

Katz expected the pain and knew he would have to overcome it if he were to avenge himself while he could.

"Traitorous son of a bitch." He spit the words as he swung the Uzi toward Lukes.

"Katz, don't!" Manning threw himself at his chief's gun, deflecting a shot that streaked harmlessly skyward.

Struggling to retain his balance, Katz followed Manning's pointed finger.

At the rim of the hill a figure was sinking slowly to his knees. A gun fell from his hand as he collapsed.

"Nahib Kamal? Sadam's lieutenant?"

"Yeah. Lukes just saved your ass. Come on. Get us out of here."

"Thanks," Katz told him. "Keep this up and we might get out alive."

Unscathed by the runaway vehicles, growing masses of the militia were charging up the hill. In the dark, unable to comprehend what was happening, they were bent on attacking someone.

To save Sadam. To avenge him. To experience the exhilarating catharsis of battle.

But they were coming, ready to kill, ready to capture the American Vice President. Ready for anything.

"Katz." Encizo had joined them.

He didn't ask. He didn't have to. Katz knew the question. He figured the answer.

"Shoot up the hill," he said.

They hesitated. Had they heard right?

He swung his weapon up and to the left and fired into the empty ruins there. Manning followed his lead. Then Encizo and Major Allen Lukes. The muzzle blasts pointed the way.

Katz shouted in what Arabic he knew. The others gestured wildly and started running ahead of the militia. Encizo spun and fell as if he was hit. He screamed in agony. Katz knelt as if to help. Manning and the major also fell.

They were nearly stomped and kicked in the stampede, but not everyone fell for the ruse. Katz killed two men who seemed to catch on to the deception.

With the scene dissolving into fevered delirium, the team headed for the helicopter. Before they reached it, their trick had lost some of its persuasiveness.

"Don't shoot back," Katz yelled. "Just run like hell."

Darting and sprinting, changing directions, even rolling over the ground, they were taking minor hits and spilling some blood. But they were alive, no more than thirty yards from the chopper. Then Katz caught a glimpse over his shoulder of two Lebanese who had dropped to the ground and were readying one calm, well-aimed stream of fire.

Katz stopped. He was going to give the pair one choice target and see if he could beat them.

A line of tracers streaked past his knees. They did not come from the Sadamites but, rather, from the direction of the helicopter.

The two militiamen on the ground tried to escape. One never got to his feet. He died where he lay. The other dived over the hill.

Katz, running parallel to the tracers, reached the helicopter and ducked to avoid the blades that were surging toward takeoff speed.

At his feet was Stephen Shaw. He was proudly looking down the sights of the heavy-caliber machine gun that he had used to save Katz and perhaps more of his rescuers.

"Vietnam," he said. "I wasn't always a politician."

Katz pulled him to his feet, slapped him on the shoulder, then grabbed McCarter by the wrist. He tried to pull the Englishman from the seat next to the pilot of the helicopter.

"Get out," he shouted, but in the roar he knew he could not be heard. He formed the words with his lips.

Motioning for the others to follow, he left the aircraft.

McCarter looked stunned. He got out, considered shooting the pilot and settled for catching up to his friends instead.

The chopper engines went to full power; it began to lift. Before it was twenty feet from the ground, Sadam's foundlings were firing at it, convinced that someone was escaping.

Twenty yards away, Katz swung into the saddle of the old Harley. The Vice President took the rear seat.

With the others alongside, they sped off. Behind them, the boys were running down the hills. They had had enough action for one day.

A few of the enemy were taking up the pursuit of those on the motorcycles. Katz devised a plan for them.

"Shoot at the helicopter," he told his passenger.

Shaw freed one hand and started shooting. The others fired when they could.

Their pursuers fell for Katz's last trump card. The Lebanese assumed those on the motorcycles were also locals, that the escaping enemy must be in the helicopter.

Carloads of local gangs were shooting at the helicopter, too.

Katz looked up. The Vice President was too good. His bullets were chipping away at the passenger section.

"For God's sake, don't shoot it down. If he's headed where I would under the circumstances, we can shoot at him all the way to the Israeli border. It'll keep the militia off our backs."

Finally, the other vehicles slowed down and turned around. They had gone beyond their usual turf.

Only God knew, come morning, who would be battling whom.

Phoenix Force—bonded in secrecy to avenge the acts of terrorists everywhere.

Super Phoenix Force #2

American "killer" mercenaries are involved in a KGB plot to overthrow the government of a South Pacific island. The American President, anxious to preserve his country's image and not disturb the precarious position of the island nation's government, sends in the experts—Phoenix Force—to prevent a coup.

Available now at your favorite retail outlet, or reserve your copy for shipping by sending your name, address, zip or postal code along with a check or money order for $4.70 (includes 75¢ for postage and handling) payable to Gold Eagle Books:

In the U.S.

Gold Eagle Books
901 Fuhrmann Blvd.
Box 1325
Buffalo, NY 14269-1325

In Canada

Gold Eagle Books
P.O. Box 609
Fort Erie, Ontario
L2A 5X3

Please specify book title with your order.

SPF-2A

From Europe to Africa, the Executioner stalks his elusive enemy—a cartel of ruthless men who might prove too powerful to defeat.

DON PENDLETON's
MACK BOLAN
Moving Target

One of America's most powerful corporations is reaping huge profits by dealing in arms with anyone who can pay the price. Dogged by assassins, Mack Bolan follows his only lead fast and hard—and becomes caught up in a power struggle that might be his last.

Available now at your favorite retail outlet, or reserve your copy for shipping by sending your name, address, zip or postal code along with a check or money order for $4.70 (includes 75¢ for postage and handling) payable to Gold Eagle Books to:

In the U.S.	In Canada
Gold Eagle Books	Gold Eagle Books
901 Fuhrmann Blvd.	P.O. Box 609
Box 1325	Fort Erie, Ontario
Buffalo, NY 14269-1325	L2A 5X3

Please specify book title with your order.

SB-14A

Nile Barrabas's most daring mission is about to begin...

JACK HILD

An explosive situation is turned over to a crack commando squad led by Nile Barrabas when a fanatical organization jeopardizes the NATO alliance by fueling public unrest and implicating the United States and Russia in a series of chemical spills.

Available in April at your favorite retail outlet, or reserve your copy for March shipping by sending your name, address, zip or postal code along with a check or money order for $4.70 (includes 75¢ for postage and handling) payable to Gold Eagle Books:

In the U.S.

Gold Eagle Books
901 Fuhrmann Blvd.
Box 1325
Buffalo, NY 14269-1325

In Canada

Gold Eagle Books
P.O. Box 609
Fort Erie, Ontario
L2A 5X3

Please specify book title with your order.

SBA-3

TAKE 'EM NOW

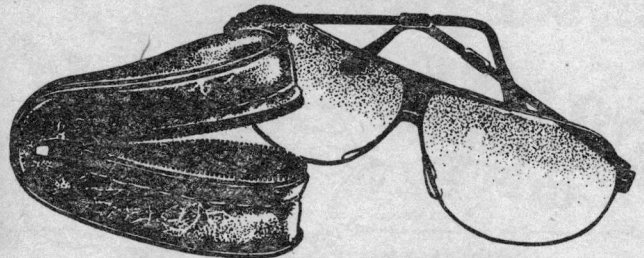

FOLDING SUNGLASSES FROM GOLD EAGLE

Mean up your act with these tough, street-smart shades. Practical, too, because they fold 3 times into a handy, zip-up polyurethane pouch that fits neatly into your pocket. Rugged metal frame. Scratch-resistant acrylic lenses. Best of all, they can be yours for only $6.99.

MAIL YOUR ORDER TODAY.

Send your name, address, and zip code, along with a check or money order for just $6.99 + .75¢ for postage and handling (for a total of $7.74) payable to Gold Eagle Reader Service. (New York and Iowa residents please add applicable sales tax.)

Remove from pouch...

unfold once...

Gold Eagle Reader Service
901 Fuhrmann Blvd.
P.O. Box 1396
Buffalo, N.Y. 14240-1396

unfold twice...

and they're ready to wear.

Offer not available in Canada.

TAKE 'EM FREE
4 action-packed novels plus a mystery bonus

NO RISK NO OBLIGATION TO BUY

SPECIAL LIMITED-TIME OFFER

Mail to Gold Eagle Reader Service®

In the U.S.
P.O. Box 1394
Buffalo, N.Y. 14240-1394

In Canada
P.O. Box 609
Fort Erie, Ont. L2A 5X3

YEAH! Rush me 4 free Gold Eagle novels and my free mystery bonus. Then send me 6 brand-new novels every other month as they come off the presses. Bill me at the low price of just $14.94—an 11% saving off the retail price - plus 95¢ postage and handling per shipment. There is no minimum number of books I must buy. I can always return a shipment and cancel at any time. Even if I never buy another book from Gold Eagle, the 4 free novels and the mystery bonus are mine to keep forever.

166 BPM BP8S

Name _____ (PLEASE PRINT)

Address _____ Apt. No. _____

City _____ State/Prov. _____ Zip/Postal Code _____

Signature (If under 18, parent or guardian must sign)

This offer is limited to one order per household and not valid to present subscribers. Price is subject to change.

TE-SUB-1DR